SEVEN DEADLY PENS

Thriller, fantasy and mystery stories to keep you up all night

STEVE MORETTI   K. BRADLEY   DAVID DEVINE
MATT C. SULLY   LARA BUJOLD CLOUDEN   PETER SMITH
MERJA TAMMI

Copyright

Seven Deadly Pens
by the KFC Scrutineers

Cover Design: Travis Gobeil

Copyright © 2022 by Steve Moretti, K. Bradley, David Devine, Matt C. Sully, Lara Bujould Clouden, Peter Smith and Merja Tammi. (The KFC Scrutineers)

All rights reserved. *(v. 1.0)* No part of this book may be reproduced in any form or by any electronic or mechanical means, including information storage and retrieval systems, without written permission from the authors, except for the use of brief quotations in a book review.

Published by DWA Media - Ottawa, Canada

SEVEN DEADLY PENS

Andy and the Time Slip App *(Steve Moretti)*
Andy had a very good life until temptation got the best of him one day. But if he can rewind time, is he free to break the rules again?

Brisé *(K. Bradley)*
Six-year-old Abigail lives amid the safety of her grandparent's farm until a stranger beckons her to the abandoned house across the field. Though forbidden to enter, Abigail senses the truth of her family's dark past may be waiting inside.

Tommy Gun *(David Devine)*
You give them clear instructions at gunpoint, and they do the opposite. It's a death sentence written by their own actions. They have no one to blame but themselves.

Voices in the Void *(Matt C. Sully)*
When Singh 12-b is struck by an unknown disaster, Starseed engineers Graham and Park are isolated from family and crew, desperate to survive, and terrified to discover the truth behind the planet's destruction.

The Thing with Feathers *(Lara Bujold Clouden)*
Another new school. Another town. An unstable mother. Its makes anyone a little crazy, so when supernatural beings

begin to appear, Jen is left wondering: Are things getting better, or much, much, worse?

The Cursed Memory *(Peter Smith)*
　　Imagine the ability to remember everything: the good, the bad, and the deadly.

Walking after Midnight *(Merja Tammi)*
　　Detective Koski had his man, but an inexperienced prosecutor and a flimsy lie allowed the killer to go free. Now a vigilante killer is doing what Martin couldn't. Should he pursue the case or let the vigilante do his worst?

Contents

Acknowledgement	vii
Introduction	ix
Andy and The Time Slip App *Steve Moretti*	1
Brisé *K. Bradley*	27
Tommy Gun *David Devine*	57
Voices in the Void *Matt C. Sully*	67
The Thing wth Feathers *Lara Bujold Clouden*	107
The Cursed Memory *Peter Smith*	125
Walking After Midnight *Merja Tammi*	153
Please leave a review!	173
About the KFC Scrutineers	175

Acknowledgement

The KFC Scurtineers writing group extends our sincere thanks to **Steve Moretti** for his vision and efforts in producing this anthology.

Seven Deadly Pens is a collaboration of creativity that came together as a cohesive work through Steve's dedication, knowledge and organized leadership.

About the art

Special thanks to **Travis Gobeil** for his cover design and for the creation of the images that introduce each story in this collection. Thank you Travis!

Please check out his website, **travisgobeil.ca** for more information on Travis and his design services.

Introduction

Turn the lights down low, make a cup of your favourite brew and get tucked in for seven page-turning short stories from the KFC Scrutineers writing group.

The stories include thriller, mystery, science fiction and fantasy tales, all with deadly consequences.

This is the group's first short story anthology. Watch for another batch of stories later this year!

Andy and the Time Slip App

Steve Moretti

Andy had a very good life until temptation got the best of him one day. But if he can rewind time, is he free to break the rules again?

Andy and the Time Slip App
Steve Moretti

"Did you hear a single word I said, Andy?"

"What?"

Andy Jones fiddled with his phone a while longer, then finally looked up.

His wife Cindy stood in the kitchen behind a mountain of plates, cutlery, party decorations and a line-up of colourful wine and liquor bottles standing at attention like soldiers preparing to storm the beaches of sobriety.

"The kids have a little surprise for you. Something they've been planning for your birthday since they got home from school for the summer." Cindy struggled to lift a heavy cooler up onto the kitchen island counter. "Their friends are going to help them with the instruments and amps."

"Amps?"

"Yeah. They're going to do a whole set of that heavy metal reggae you like. I let them rent lights and whatever they needed." Cindy unwrapped a brown paper package and with two hands carried it around the counter.

Cindy held the ruby red mountain of meat in front of Andy, beaming as if she had birthed it herself. "Look at this prime rib! Seven ribs. It's nine kilos, almost twenty pounds! Going to take a while on the grill. Do you know if we have enough propane?"

"Propane?"

Cindy set down the heavy roast and sighed. "What's wrong?" Her furrowed eyebrows tightened. "You don't seem excited at all. It's a beautiful day, the kids are setting up the pool and the backyard… it's going to be quite a party."

She pulled up a chair beside him and laid her hand over his. "And after everyone's gone, you and I…" she winked, lowering her voice, "can have our own little party."

Andy forced a smile. Cindy was trying so hard. Why couldn't he be more enthusiastic?

"Sorry, Cin," he sighed. "I'm just so worried about work. We have the launch for the new app next week and…"

He couldn't tell her much more because he didn't understand it himself. He was the head of R&D, although the job was more managing egocentric engineers than leading the research. Still, he'd logged many years at the top of his game as an innovator. But damn if he could make sense of this new system. What started as an entertainment / mental health app, like digital tarot cards for improving memory functions, had morphed into something quite different.

"My team is burned out, and I just got the new prototype wristband last night from the professor in Bulgaria, the guy that invented this thing." He touched his wrist. "Jill's got the conference centre booked for over a thousand people, and she needs new screenshots for her slide deck, but…"

He glanced down at his phone. "I think we need to wait and do more testing."

Cindy nodded, lifting her hands from his and brushing a hand through her strawberry blonde hair. She looked as tired as he felt. "Well, the kids and I, and all our friends are coming over today to celebrate with you. Can you not just let it go,

Andy? Tomorrow you're going to be fifty years old! Today, you need to have fun, the last day before you start slobbering and getting all senile on me!"

She stood up and gave him a peck on the cheek. "I've got a million things to get ready. Oh, and I almost forgot. I emailed you some links where we can go next year for our twenty-fifth. What do you think of Greece?"

"Do they have Wi-Fi?"

"Andy!" she scolded with a gentle laugh. "Go check the propane."

"Propane's fine, Cin," Andy mumbled after returning to the kitchen.

He touched his phone again while Cindy continued with her preparations. As she worked on finishing another tray of her mini caprese cherry tomato skewers, she babbled on excitedly about places she'd been researching for their wedding anniversary next year. Greece, Portugal and even the Maldives seemed to be under serious consideration.

Maybe it would sound fun in a week or two when he had the mental space to think about it. But for now, what was he supposed to do about the app and this theoretical 'time slip' technology he'd been testing? Had he just dreamed that he went back and forth in time like he was casually flipping through channels on his TV remote, re-living his first overwhelming day as an engineering undergrad, and the painful night when he broke up with his college sweetheart?

He slid his finger over the opening screen of the app: TimeSlip v.09 (beta), by Chronosoft. *The times of your life.* It was timed release with a hard-coded expiry.

Jill, the head of the marketing team, had crafted the tagline, but did she have any idea this was more than just a novelty app? The one-eyed professor Vanyo Petrova claimed he decoded the overlooked footnotes in the equations of Albert Einstein. Andy's engineering team had given up studying the architectural schematics inside Vanyo's prototype titanium wrist band.

And, apart from Petrova, no one understood how the 'TimeBand' worked.

Somehow, it derived power through contact with skin. Its main component was an unstable isotope of Technetium and showed traces of radioactivity. Andy tried to warn his boss, Bjorn, the CEO of Chronosoft, that hardware certification would be virtually impossible, but he told Andy to focus on finalizing the software for the TimeBand.

The blustering CEO joked that he would handle the 'nervous Nellie' bureaucrats.

Next Wednesday, after Bjorn unveiled the TimeSlip app, he was taking Chronosoft public. A few technical hiccups, he explained, were minor details compared to the life-changing wealth generated by the one hundred and eighty million shares being offered through the IPO. The offering price per share had already tripled through intense media coverage of the project.

"You have to take a seaplane to get to this one resort in the Maldives," Cindy explained as she finished off the first row of skewers and reached for more fresh basil. "It's a private island. Every room is on the beach. Some are even right on the water."

"Uh-huh," Andy mumbled as he worried about Wednesday.

How could he possibly approve the wristband and the app before then, when the national media circus came to town? Was his last troubling timeslip experience just a fluke? How could Andy make sure that Bjorn understood the implications of this technology before he bound onstage to do his usual *schtick* in front of two thousand people and a world-wide streaming audience?

Andy adjusted the TimeBand on his wrist and the TimeSlip app finally connected. He confirmed his phone's Bluetooth pairing with the device and clicked on the app's preference settings.

"Good," he muttered.

Cindy was explaining the options at the Maldives resort. "Yoga, fitness, spa, sailing, diving…"

"That sounds great, hon." Andy slid his finger across the screen to the TimeSlip preference settings. A slider allowed the user to select a range: 'Birth-21,' 'Teen Years,' or 'Any Decade' with a drop-down to select the user's preferred decade.

There was also one other option: 'Birth-TVE+' with a red information button beside it. He touched it.

'The Very End. Plus'

Below the title was scrolling paragraphs of legal text. He scrolled through it all and clicked 'ACCEPT.' The TimeBand tightened around his wrist. The app preferences were now set and the TimeSlip options greyed out.

"Cindy!" an excited voice startled him.

"Hey Jill," Cindy replied, covering the tray of appetizers with clear wrap, and opening the double door fridge, already stuffed with food for the party. "Finally, I get some real help."

"No problem, just put me to work," Jill replied, and turned toward Andy. "Is the birthday boy ready to *parrrr-teee?*"

Andy smiled. "Yeah, of course."

Jill and her husband had just moved in last month, right across the street. Her outfit made Andy look away and stare down at his feet, before daring to a steal another glance. Jill was squeezed into a candy red bikini, with white sandals and pink sunglasses pushed up high over her dyed platinum hair. A saucy black sarong with tassels was loosely wrapped around her waist. Her bare, tanned thigh peeked through the sarong hanging provocatively between her legs.

"Hope you don't mind, Cin," Jill smiled, still staring at Andy. "Just went for a dip in your pool. Water's *soooo* nice!"

Cindy laughed. "Glad somebody's enjoying it. The old man here is being a grump." She walked over and fluffed Andy's dark blonde mop top. "Maybe you should go for a swim too." His wife leaned closer and planted a kiss on his cheek. "You need to get happy, hon!"

She's right, Andy sighed. He *was* still a young man – for one more day at least. Tomorrow he would officially be fifty freaking years old.

GUESTS STARTED ARRIVING MID-AFTERNOON. Andy's kids Cameron and Olivia, plus a collection of their friends from university and around the neighbourhood, were busy setting up drums, guitars, amps, and other equipment. They took turns pumping out tunes from their phones, mixing the music up nicely, including plenty of Andy's old favourites.

Cindy had asked if he could get the barbeque going, and he was thankful to have a task. Yeah, it was his party, but he wasn't ready to celebrate the dawning of middle age quite yet. The real issue though, was the launch of 'the app.' If it flopped next week, his days as head of Chronosoft R&D were toast.

Starting over at fifty? He was already going grey. He'd just swapped his drugstore reading glasses for a strong prescription set and he was losing the battle against an expanding waistline intent on claiming more and more territory. What's next? Trouble peeing, enlarged prostate, can't keep it up …

"Andy!" a voice crashed his pity party.

It was Bjorn, his boss. The bombastic CEO of Chronosoft, decked out in long surfer boardshorts and a teal blue company golf shirt, punched a beach ball toward Andy who tried to catch it. Instead, it sailed right past him.

Bjorn sauntered over, flashing his wall-to-wall salesman smile. "Happy Birthday, man!" he barked. "Great party! Whatcha' cooking?"

Andy raised the cover of the barbeque. The grill was crowded with a variety of mini burgers: beef, lamb, turkey, and ground shrimp. "Just some sliders for now." He flipped a few of them over. "I'm going to put the prime rib on later."

Bjorn patted Andy's back. "Everything good for Wednesday? How's the firmware and the soft —" He stopped mid-sentence, glancing down at Andy's wristband. "It's all working now?"

"Not sure, still testing."

Bjorn studied Andy's wrist. "Can I see?"

Andy raised his left hand so Bjorn could get a better look at the TimeBand. "Hmmm. The LED is flashing red. What setting are you using?"

"TVE Plus." Andy shook his wrist. "It's stuck though, I can't change it. Might have to reinstall."

"I love that 'TVE Plus' idea!" Bjorn laughed. "Jill's got such a knack for branding! 'The Very End… Plus' The investors love it. They want us to trademark it." He glanced around at a group getting ready to play water polo in the pool, then back at Andy.

"Can you kill that flashing red LED when you get a minute? Makes it look like the thing's dying and I want you to show it to the head of the teacher's pension fund over by the pool there. He's just about ready to sign off on one million shares." Bjorn held his hand out. "Mind if I take a few sliders over to him?"

After loading up Bjorn up with a plate of sliders, Andy

surveyed his backyard. People were everywhere, with more coming. Maybe it was time to mingle and talk to…

A pair of soft hands covered his eyes. "Hey stranger."

Floral notes of rose and jasmine teased his nose. Fingers gently massaged his eyes with feathery lightness.

"Guess who!" the voice whispered, wet lips touching his ear.

"I know your perfume, Jill."

"Ahhhh… no fair!" She removed her hands from Andy's face and stepped in front of him. "How come you're all alone over here?" she pouted. "Why don't you come and play in the pool with me?"

"Jill, I don't think it's a good idea." He scanned the yard for Cindy. He saw her heading back into the house carrying a tray of empty plates.

Jill pushed closer. Her bikini top struggled to contain her wet, perfectly-sculptured assets. Damp platinum hair framed her moist face as she puckered her shimmering, pink-glossed lips.

"I've got a birthday surprise for you," she cooed. "Something you've wanted a long time – a very long time."

They stood toe-to-toe, both nearly six feet tall. Dressed in sandals, shorts and a Chronosoft T-shirt, Andy despite his dread of growing old, felt like a young man. He was still in excellent health, and right now, his circulatory system was sending high octane blood to body parts that weren't ready to play dead just yet.

Working with Jill over the last year meant spending long hours together as the TimeSlip project evolved from wacky idea to reality. As the head of Marketing, she was always dropping by his office to ask how the app and hardware worked, and trying out branding and marketing ideas on him. He was okay with the long days together, but she hinted she'd like some long nights too.

Up until now he'd found excuses not to travel with her to

investor presentations out of town, trying to ignore her not-so-subtle flirtations. But he wondered if his resolve was wavering. Thankfully, Jill's husband Gord waved to him from the other side of the pool.

"Got to go, Jill."

"You up for eighteen tomorrow?" Gord asked.

Andy hesitated. "Uh well…"

"I know, I know, not too early. She's probably got a surprise or two for you tonight." Gord winked.

"She?"

"Your wife?" Gord pushed Andy. "At least that's what Jillie would do." He glanced at his watch. "Shoot! I gotta take the kids to the game, but I'll be back to help you blow out your candles, buddy."

Gord turned and began to walk away. "I'll book us a Noon tee off, so you can get your strength back old man!" he joked, waving a hand in the air as he left through the backyard gate. Gord waited for a car to pass by before hurrying across the street.

For the next hour, Andy manned the barbeque as guests made their way over to wish him a happy birthday and offer him a drink. Jill kept coming by too.

"I'm *sooooo* hot," she whispered, her wet lips on his ears testing his resistance for signs of weakness. "I know what you need," she pleaded, "the same thing I've needed… for so long."

What Andy needed was to send her away. He was in charge. He wouldn't be controlled by the primordial parts of his brainstem screaming at him to take Jill right here and now, on the picnic table by the barbeque.

"Just this once, while you're still the best-looking man at

the party." Jill's warm breath was moist in his ear. "No one will *ever* know."

Andy noticed the LED on the wristband had stopped flashing. It glowed red.

He closed his eyes. The sounds of the party faded as he repeated her words *'while you're still the best-looking man at the party.'* His mind wandered.

He heard hissing and loud booing from the audience watching the disastrous launch of the failed app. His kids laughed at him. He needed a walker to cross the street. His driver's license was refused with a red stamp: 'TOO OLD.'

Jill whispered in his ear. "Take what you want, Andy. *Everything* you've ever dreamed of…"

He grabbed her bare leg. "Okay. Let's go."

Jill squealed. "Give me five minutes."

She hurried away, slipped through the gates and across the street. He watched her leave, his heart pounding, all his senses awake and alive at last. He lifted the bloodied hunk of prime rib onto the barbeque grill, lowered the flame and closed the lid. After a couple of minutes, he wandered over to the gate, looking over his shoulder a few times. He waited a moment for traffic to clear, crossed the street, and ran toward Jill's house.

She called to him from upstairs when he opened the front door. He climbed the stairs, blood rushing to his head, ignoring the voices demanding he stop before this went any further.

Jill lay naked on her king-size bed, writhing like a creature in heat. "Come to me."

He tore off his T-shirt, pulled down his shorts and flipped off his sandals. He was in her arms in an instant, locking Jill in a deep kiss as they explored each other. Like teenagers who had worked themselves into a hormonal frenzy, they made love urgently; bucking, rolling, and then finally, screaming out together in unison.

Afterward, they lay panting, sprawled over the bed.

"Ohhhhh," he moaned.

"Andy," Jill murmured as if in a dream, "you're a beast!"

He felt a tug on his wrist. The TimeBand pulsed, then tightened. "I better go."

Andy rolled off the bed, pulled on his shirt and shorts, slipped on his sandals and left Jill's bedroom quickly without looking back. He lumbered down the stairs, eyes closed, trying not to think too much.

He suddenly felt cold.

Outside the front door, the afternoon sun had faded to dull twilight. He stood on Jill's front porch. How long had he been here?

The streetlight hummed, buzzed a few times then blinked on. He began to walk toward the street back to his house and his birthday party. He heard shouting and the music stopped. The shouting got louder. He rushed across the street.

When he finally dashed through the gate, he heard Cindy screaming. "Help him!"

Everyone was near the pool, shouting and yelling. He ran toward them, trying to push people aside so he could see, but they all ignored him. He finally got through to the edge, and then to his horror, saw that someone was lying at the bottom of his pool.

"Get him!" Cindy yelled.

Andy's son Cameron dove into the pool. He propelled himself down to the bottom of the deep end and lifted the person up to the surface of the water. Andy leaned closer for a better look. The man looked familiar; tall, slightly overweight, wearing the same colour shorts as him.

Cindy began to scream. "Is he breathing?"

Andy stared in shock at the man in his son's arm. It was his own lifeless face staring blankly back at him.

THE BLACKNESS LIFTED SLOWLY. Voices called him.

"Are you ever getting up, Andy?" his wife yelled from downstairs.

He stared up at the ceiling. Was it all just a dream?

"Andy!" Cindy called again, this time more insistent.

"Coming…" he sighed. He dragged himself out of bed, splashed his face with water, pulled on his shorts and T-shirt and padded downstairs in his sandals.

Cindy was starting on her caprese and cherry-tomato skewers. "You're up finally. I think there's still some coffee left, and then can you go check the propane?"

"Propane? Why?"

"For the party, hon. Your birthday party?" She speared another chunk of mozzarella, added a fresh basil leaf and a cherry tomato. She glanced over at him. "You forget all about it? Your last day of fun before you start slobbering and getting all senile on me! Or is it already too late?"

This was all so much like his dream. Wow…

"And if you get a chance, look at those links I sent you. Greece looks good, but I there's this resort in the Maldives on a private island. Every room is on the beach."

Something wasn't right. "Didn't you already tell me that?"

His wife laughed. "No, hon. I just found it this morning before you got up."

Andy stood staring at her. He felt something tight on his wrist. It was the TimeBand. The red LED light had faded to dull grey. He needed to find his phone and check the TimeSlip app to see if…

"Cindy!" a familiar voice startled him.

"Hey Jill," his wife sang out.

Andy froze at the sight of Jill. She wore that same intoxicating bikini and sarong outfit.

"And how's the birthday boy?" Jill giggled. "Ready to *parrr-tee*?"

"Yeah. Uh no, no… sorry, I need to find my phone."

Andy and the Time Slip App

Andy ran from the kitchen and hurried up the stairs. His phone was still charging in his bedroom. He yanked out the charging cable, touched the TimeSlip app icon and found the setting screen. It was locked on 'TVE+.' The toggle to change it was greyed out.

"What the hell?" He tried to slide it over. It wouldn't budge.

Andy ran downstairs, phone in hand and popped his head into the kitchen. Jill was helping Cindy with the appetizers. "Hey, I need to go out. I forgot something at the office."

Both women looked up at him. "Don't be long, Andy," his wife replied without looking up. Jill winked at him and smiled slyly.

He had to get out of here. Maybe someone on his team knew how to reset the app and get this damn TimeBand off his wrist.

Andy got into his car, backed onto the street and drove towards his office. The TimeBand was flashing again, bright blue this time. Was he hallucinating? Had he cheated on his wife last night? Was he still 49 years old?

He rolled to a stop at the intersection and gasped to see Cindy in a dark dress, and the kids all dressed up walking into a building on the other side of the street. The light changed as he drove ahead slowly to see where they were going. He read the sign above the building: 'McGowan Funeral Home and Chapel.'

"What the hell?" He parked his car in the side lot and checked his face in the mirror. He hadn't shaved, was dressed in shorts and a T-shirt but… he had to see what his family was doing here. No one noticed him enter the building. He looked around and saw an arrow pointing to the chapel. The doors were closed.

There was a sign outside the chapel door:

Mr. Andrew Jones

No! Really?

Slowly, he opened the door and took a few steps inside. There was a casket in the middle aisle of the chapel. People who had attended his birthday party, his parents and other family and colleagues from work, all were seated in the pews on either side.

His son Cameron, dressed in a dark suit with a tight red tie, made his way up to the front and stepped behind the podium.

"I'd like to say a few words about my dad. My mom and my sister are having a tough time, and they've asked me to try and tell you a little about him."

Cameron's voice was breaking. He cleared his throat. "Andy was not only a brilliant and gifted engineer, he was also a loving father who taught me to ride a bike, tie a Windsor knot, and shared his vintage vinyl collection with me. He coached my soccer team and never questioned when I needed to borrow money."

Andy held his throat, staring, eyes watering. Although he had moved up closer, standing near the casket in his shorts, t-shirts and sandals, no one paid him any attention.

"Same with Olivia. My dad always said his job was to spoil her. And he did a real good job at it too," Cameron, wiped his eyes, looking over at Cindy in the front row. "But it was Mom he doted on best. He loved her so much, it was like they were put on earth to find one another. They never stopped being each other's best friend. And they were so excited about celebrating their twenty-fifth wedding anniversary next year with their trip of a lifetime to Greece and the Maldives."

Andy couldn't listen anymore. He tried to pull off the wristband. It was stuck. The more he pulled, the tighter it seemed to grip his wrist. He gave up, ran out of the funeral home and drove home.

Cars lined the street and filled his driveway. He parked a

block away, walked back to the house and slipped into the front door. He called out to his wife. "Cindy?"

There was no response but there were people milling about everywhere. The men were dressed in suits and the women in long, dark dresses. He padded through his house as though he were invisible. Cindy stood in the corner of the living room talking to Jill's husband Gord.

"Apparently, he didn't drown," she said in a teary voice. "Andy tripped and hit his head on the cement edge of the deck, then fell in the pool, probably already unconscious according to the coroner."

"Jill and I are so sorry," Gord replied. "I know how good a man he was, always going on and on about how great you were, while we were all complaining about our wives." His face was tightly drawn. "He loved you so much."

Cindy batted away tears. "I know, I know. I just wished I had told him, one last time, that he was my whole world."

Andy couldn't take this. He tugged again at the TimeBand, vainly trying to extract the horrible device from his wrist. It would not let go. He ran upstairs, flung himself on his bed and let the world go dark.

WHEN HIS EYES FLUTTERED OPEN, Andy blinked up at the ceiling. Bright sunshine streamed through his bedroom window.

"You getting up, Andy?" Cindy was calling him to come downstairs.

He sat up on the bed. The TimeBand was blinking again, green. There must be some logic to these colours, he thought. He reached for his phone and checked the date. It was the day of his birthday party. Again.

What did it all mean? Was he Bill Murray in *Groundhog Day*?

"I'm going to take a shower," he yelled down, turning things over in his head. He let the hot water soothe his aching back, rejuvenating and refreshing his whole body. "You're okay," he coached himself. "You can handle this. Just go with it."

When he was done his shower, Andy searched for a different shirt, a light green one with a collar and long knee-length shorts.

Downstairs in the kitchen Cindy was cleaning up the counter. "Look at this prime rib," she gushed. "Seven ribs –"

"Nine kilos right, almost twenty pounds?" he interrupted.

"Yeah!" she grinned. "Smartypants!"

He was about to give her a hug when an alert on his phone beeped.

"People keep sending you birthday messages," Cindy said.

Andy reached for his phone. The alert was a message pop up: "TimeSlip beta expires soon."

Really? Maybe that's it, he thought nodding his head. *I'll just let it expire and get my life back. Just play it cool and things will be*

"Cindy!" The one voice he didn't want to hear.

"Hey Jill." His wife sang out. He had to get out of here before…

"And how's the birthday boy? Ready to–"

"*Parrrr-teee*? Hell yeah!" He grinned, walking over to his wife to give her a big wet kiss.

"Shoooo," Cindy laughed, pushing him away. "Go away! You old man!" She opened the fridge. "I've got to finish these appetizers. Go check the propane."

Cindy took out another container of fresh mozzarella and put it on the counter. "Jill, can you go with him and make sure he doesn't get distracted?"

"Can do!" Jill smiled. "You can't leave that boy unsupervised you know."

Andy shook his head. "I've got to go check something

first." He stumbled out of the kitchen over to the ground-floor laundry room. He felt another alert vibrating on his phone.

YouTube: TimeSlip keynote presentation replay

Replay? He clicked the alert. In a few moments the video started to play. He closed the door to the laundry room and turned up the sound.

Clouds of dry ice rolled across the stage of the conference centre. Lights flashed inside the fog. Jill must have listened to his ideas for the music. A sample of the *2001: A Space Odyssey* theme began to play. The ominous fanfare soon gave away to 'Time is on My Side' by the Rolling Stones and then finally the bouncy riffs of the Huey Lewis hit 'Back in Time' from *Back to the Future*.

Then it all morphed into an hypnotic dance rhythm as bright spotlights began to circle the stage.

"Wow..." Andy whispered. This app might pose an existential threat to humanity, but damn, what an opening!

He watched as the music faded, the dry ice evaporated, and a booming voice introduced the speaker. "Ladies and gentlemen, members of the media and to the millions watching around the world, it's my pleasure to introduce the visionary product pioneer, the breakaway medical scientist, the fastest code junkie on Earth, and a chess grandmaster to boot!"

Music began pounding in the irresistible *stomp, stomp, clap – stomp, stomp, clap* rhythm of Queen's 'We Will Rock You.' Lights flashed in time with the beat as the audience stomped, clapped, hooted and hollered.

"Please give a warm welcome to a man beyond his time, the Chairman and CEO of Chronosoft, Mr. Bjoorrrrrrnn-nnnn Olson!"

To wild applause, strobe lights and cheering, Bjorn ran

onto the stage. He raised a hand and held it high until the audience began to settle and then went completely quiet.

"Time no longer lives *only* in the past," he announced. "All you need is one of these," he raised up a cell phone, "and a Chronosoft TimeBand!" The blackness of the monstrous screen behind him dissolved into an image of the wristband slowly rotating in outer space in a sea of stars and coloured galaxies. "And, the free app we are releasing at one minute after midnight, Greenwich Mean Time – TimeSlip 1.0!"

To the familiar orchestral strains of the Jupiter movement from Gustav Holst's 'The Planets,' the audience began cheering until Bjorn raised his hand to quiet them one more time. He was both feeding, and *feeding off*, the crowd's energy.

"Our proprietary algorithm combines your DNA markers with your medical, and family history, internet footprint and most importantly, information from the Chronosoft TimeBand. It harvests the electrical currents flowing within your body to extract residual, high-resolution memories. Imagine re-living the best moments of life over and over or, slipping ahead using our predictive neural network to see what awaits you."

The audience hushed.

Andy shook his head. He'd given Jill some of this information, even though he didn't understand half of what Vanyo Petrova explained about the TimeBand. It supposedly fused with the user's skin to operate as a 'wetware' computer harnessing the dynamic nature of the eighty billion neurons in the human brain. No one in the audience questioned the science. Everyone remained enraptured with Bjorn as he came to the conclusion of his presentation.

"And so, my friends, as of this day, you can now timeslip through your life. From the moment of conception to the very end, through a setting we call 'TVE Plus.' Your whole life is waiting for you to experience from beginning to end, and even a little bit after, 'the end'."

Indoor pyrotechnics began, and the music rose up once more. There was a sharp knock on the laundry door as the crowd rose to its feet.

"Andy? You in there?" Cindy called.

He clicked his phone off and opened the door. "Yeah, sorry, just had to watch something…"

"It's okay. I know it's for work," she said, holding a large platter "But can you get these sliders going on the barbeque?"

WHILE HIS KIDS warmed up with the band and cranked out some of his favourite tunes on their PA system, Andy flipped the mini burgers. He was lost in thought, not sure what was real anymore. His son Cameron came over, asked if he had any other song requests, and left with a tray of sliders for his sister Olivia and their friends.

As Cameron walked away, a pair of hands covered his eyes. "Hey, stranger."

Oh no. Not again.

"Jill, please," Andy replied, grabbing her slender wrists and pulling her arms down. She pressed into him. The feel of her sumptuous body, the fresh memory of their fervid sexual encounter, and that bewitching perfume dabbled behind her ears, all conspired to challenge his resolve.

He froze as she continued to grind into him. "I know the way you look at me," she whispered. "Why fight it?"

Andy closed his eyes. She was like a chemical addiction, a guilty pleasure he loathed but was somehow powerless to resist.

But what about Cindy and his kids? He needed to be the man they thought he was. "No, Jill," he replied sternly. "It's not going to happen."

She smiled. "Oh, I like that look on you, when you take

control. Go ahead, own me, every square inch of me, from top to bottom, and back!"

Jill grazed his lips with hers and sauntered back to the pool.

He stood watching the sway of her body, a bucket of testosterone coursing through his veins. He glanced at his wristband. It pulsed red again.

He stared at Jill, flaunting herself in the pool. He stared a long time, remembering the feel of her naked body beneath him.

For the next hour he tried to ignore her, but she returned to flirt every fifteen minutes or so. When her husband Gord waved him over, Andy shook his head, pointing to his watch. If he was right, Gord would realize he had to leave for his kid's game.

Sure enough, after a few minutes, Gord hurried out the gate and across the street, just as had done last time.

And then, as he suspected she would, Jill shuffled over from the pool and stood beside him. She was still dripping from the pool as she leaned over and cooed in his ear. "I'm *soooo* —"

"Stop it!" He snapped. "Why can't you leave me alone? I'm married for Christ's sake!"

"Oh God..." Jill purred. "You make me weak when you talk like that. I can't go another moment without you."

Andy stared at this... this, what was she? His brazen timeslip temptress? All his weaknesses rolled into one? He checked the TimeBand. It glowed solid red.

"Andy, take what belongs to you!" She placed her wet fingers on his lips. "My body is your temple."

No one at the party seemed to notice. Cindy was shuttling drinks and appetizers back and forth. The kids were laughing with their friends, going over the show they were going to play tonight. Everyone else seemed to be having a great time at his birthday party.

Having a great time. Again.

This had all happened before. He had gone across the street with Jill to have some of the most feral sex of his life. And now, here he was, back again as if nothing had happened. And regardless of what he did, his wife and kids still loved him.

So, why was he hesitating?

Jill took his hand. "I'm going to my house to wait for you. Are you coming?"

ANDY STOOD at the edge of the street a few minutes later. He imagined Jill waiting in her bed – naked, desperate to have him.

The party raged on in his backyard. No one knew he had slipped away. The prime rib was on the grill, just like before. He felt for his phone in his pocket. Traffic streamed by in both directions.

Andy watched, unable to decide. The wristband still glowed red.

"Screw it!" he shouted and stepped onto the road.

He stopped halfway across. Whatever he did, he was probably going to die tonight. And tomorrow, he might be right back here, no one the wiser.

Andy glanced over at Jill's house. Then turned around to his own backyard. And then back at Jill's place.

He wanted to be with Jill, but a spike of guilt rose within him. Everyone thought he was a loving husband and a dedicated father. No matter what he did, they would remember him fondly.

The only person he couldn't fool was himself.

But he had to try.

Why couldn't he have it all?

He spun around toward Jill's house but tripped in his

sandals and fell onto the road just as a dump truck came barreling around the bend in the road, unable to stop in time, its air horn blasting into the night sky.

A second before the heavy truck tires flattened Andy into the pavement, the phone inside his pocket vibrated with one final alert:

The beta version of TimeSlip has expired.

About Steve Moretti

I am drawn to the passion of creativity in whatever form it takes, and equally fascinated by the mysteries of the universe with special affection for music, the universal conduit of human emotion.

My writing journey started in broadcast journalism, public relations, and advertising, then continued into educational software development while running a company I founded and ran for twenty years.

Now I concentrate most of my time on writing historical time slip fantasies, with one series complete, **Song for a Lost Kingdom** and the first novel in a new trilogy, **Michael Angelo & the Stone Mistress,** just released

I also co-authored a biographical work on composer Pyotr Ilyich Tchaikovsky entitled **Pyotr** which explores key moments in his difficult life.

I grew up in London, Ontario and also lived in Pompano Beach, Florida as a teenager. I moved to Ottawa to attend Carleton University many years ago and now live just south of the city with my wife and a fountain pen full of words.

Please visit my website, stevemorett.ca for information on all my books and audiobooks. You can also download a FREE copy of my novella prequel to the *Song for a Lost Kingdom* series here.

Brisé
K. Bradley

Six-year-old Abigail lives amid the safety of her grandparents' farm until a stranger beckons her to the abandoned house across the fields. Though forbidden to enter, Abigail senses the truth of her family's dark past may be waiting inside.

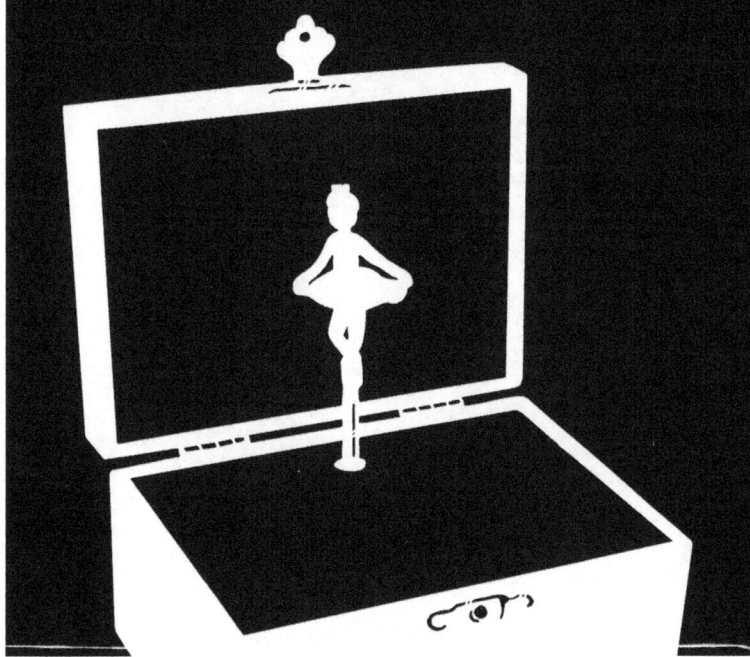

Brisé, also called Pas Brisé – French.
A classical ballet term meaning 'broken' (broken step)

Brisé

K. Bradley

Abigail pats down the pleats of her puffy skirt, enabling a view of her white patent leather shoes. She reaches forward, heeding the uncertainty of Grandpa's wooden porch swing, and touches the polished smoothness of her toes. Staring at the sparkle stamped gold writing on the bottom of her shoe, she grins and slides her finger into the small gap between the sole and the heel. Abigail has never worn a shoe with a heel before. But she's never been a flower girl either.

Butterflies dance in her tummy. They erupted in waves from the moment she opened her eyes this morning. Today is Lyla's wedding and Abigail has so much to remember. She has to keep her dress clean, her violet sash shiny side out, and the bow tied to perfection. She has to walk down the aisle. The thought of it causes the butterflies' wings to beat like hummingbirds. Lyla has shown her how: Go slowly. Step, together, step, together. Grandma has demonstrated tossing the purple petals: Gently, just a few, toss don't throw. Step, together, step, together, toss don't throw. Abigail closes her eyes, imagining her feet moving the right way as the petals fall like fairy dust. But the butterflies turn cartwheels, and she pictures the wedding guests' faces, staring.

She looks ahead to the rusty barn. It is off in the distance past the fields where corn stalks stand in tidy lines. Beyond that, made tiny by the distance, is the shadow of the brown house. Every day she looks at the brown house. She longs to see it up close. She imagines how it looks inside. The kitchen probably smells like Grandma's bread. She imagines a little girl lives there with her family. Her room has pink painted walls and white lace curtains that float against soft breezes.

She calculates how long it would take to walk there. She has had no luck counting her steps. It takes twelve steps to get to Grandpa's shed but that doesn't help at all. The rusty barn must be a million steps away and the brown house looks even farther than that.

Like every day, as she watches the brown house and imagines its insides, he appears. Today he walks toward her from a corridor of corn to her left. She is relieved. For today, like most days when the sun's warm glow creates a golden tapestry across the corn, he is a boy, a teenager. And today, like all those bright days, he smiles and waves.

But sometimes on other days, when corn sways in darkness awaiting showers from looming clouds overhead, he does not come as a boy. Those days, he comes as the wolf and stares with yellow eyes as his jaw parts and lips recede. Those days, Abi backs away from the rumbling growls and flashes of light on his shining fangs. Still, she returns the next day, to stare at the brown house and hopes for the boy.

Regardless of how he comes, she blinks, and he is gone again. And today is no exception.

The porch door creaks.

"Hey, that's where you got to." Lyla sits in Grandpa's relaxing spot and smells like Grandma's vanilla cookies. Her long, blonde hair has been swirled with tiny white flowers and silver ribbon. Abigail notices the small flash of a white satin bra strap beneath her pink polka dot bathrobe. "You look so beautiful! I'm putting on my dress. Do you want to help?"

———

GRANDMA HAS GONE QUIET, like she sometimes does. She stares at Lyla's reflection in the oval mirror. Grandma pulls her fist into her chin, holding back those tears, the ones that sometimes happen when she doesn't know Abigail is watching. Sequins flash from Lyla's dress against the sunlight that spills through the window causing Abigail to turn her head. There on the bed, Lyla's suitcases are open. The butterflies flap. Abigail flees.

"Abi?" Grandma cries "Abi, where are you going?"

The soles of the new shoes slip against the carpet on the stairs, but Abi grasps the railing and manages to stay upright to the bottom before flying out the front door. Down the steps and onto the unpaved walkway she runs, her skirt flouncing left and right with each step as the midday sun sears her bare shoulders.

"Earl, Earl! Go and get Abi!" Grandma's voice is fading as Abigail runs past the gladiolas. They watch like soldiers but are unable to stop her as she thrusts her body forward, faster and faster. At the bottom of the laneway, where Grandpa's pickup truck stands askew is the furthest point she is allowed. She turns to the right onto the gravel road that parallels the highway. She can feel her perfect ringlets dampening and knows the perfect gold letters on the soles of her shoes are being scuffed against the rough stones.

Darting through the leaf patterns dancing on the path, her tears fall, but through their mist she sees him and stops dead in mid step.

It is the boy and not the wolf and she is no afraid. He stands with one leg bent, the sole of his foot pressing into the side of a wise old elm tree. His hair is the red of a raggedy

Andy doll, and he grips a long reed between grinning Chicklet gum teeth.

"Hey there you are." He straightens his overall straps and tips the brim of his baseball cap.

Abigail places her hands on her waist; the smoothness of her violet sash sends a wave of guilt.

"It's okay," he continues, "Do you remember me?"

The butterflies take flight in every nerve of her body. "Jay?"

"Yes. Don't worry little girl. I won't hurt you. Are you lost? What's your name?"

Abigail, looks at his kind face. "I'm not lost." She musters her firmest voice. He has never been this close before. "But I can't talk to strangers." She turns to head home but her shoes seem lodged in the gravel.

"Am I a stranger? No, you're right. You are smart. How about if I promise not to come any closer? I'll just stay right here like I'm stuck to this tree." He points his hip toward the tree bark and pretends to pour glue then affixes his hip to the tree trunk. "See, now I'm stuck here. I can't leave the tree so I can't hurt you. Why are you all dressed up like that? You sure look pretty."

"My Grandpa's right behind me" She wishes it so. "I have to go."

"Where?"

She stares back at him.

"Where do you have to go, Abi?" He asks.

"To my sister's wedding."

"What's your sister's name?" His deep blue eyes sparkle.

"Lyla."

"How old are you? How old is your sister?" he asks.

"Six," she pauses and scratches at a scab on her arm from her bike tumble last week. "Lyla is twenty-one. How old are you?" She grows more confident, less afraid of him -- more afraid of Grandma and Grandpa's reaction.

Brisé

"Somewhere in between, I suppose." He laughs. "Well, Abi, I think your Mom and Dad will be looking for you. Are you sure you're not lost?"

She nods. "I just live over there." She points back toward the farmhouse.

"Oh yeah, I live over here." He points in the opposite direction.

"I know. You live in the brown house. I live with Grandma and Grandpa, and Lyla. But Lyla's leaving." A tear escapes over her lashes.

"Oh. Where are your Mom and Dad?"

She interlaces her fingers and bites her lip. She can hear Grandma's voice in her head. *It's none of anyone's business. No one in this town gets to talk about our family*. Regardless, Abi blurts "My Mom is in heaven, with my brothers."

She utters it so simply, as though the whole world doesn't know. She has never said it out loud before, not to Grandma or Lyla or even Dr. Shipley.

The glue keeping Jay against the tree has vanished. He moves toward her. She is startled by the movement and the rustling of birds in the branches.

"Sorry. I forgot." He turns back to the tree, demonstrating re-gluing himself. "And your Dad?"

She lifts her head toward the lanky young man as her eyes well with tears. Her heart races.

"My Daddy died too." She gulps "But he didn't go to heaven."

GRANDPA SAYS ONLY five words "You needed to behave today!" It was long after she'd left Jay to head back home. She meets Grandpa head-on. His red face stares her down as she awaits the worst. But instead, he reaches his oversized hand toward her, and she cautiously places her tiny fingers inside it. They walk slowly home, like an image on a greeting card: The girl in the puffy dress hand in hand with the hunched-over man in the navy suit. His eyes focus only on the grand sky ahead, his silence louder than any scolding he could utter.

In the time she's been gone, the farmhouse has erupted in gales of laughter and violet satin. Lyla's bridesmaids scurry about, posing for a plump photographer who seems obsessed with fixing stray tendrils or dabbing polished lips. Lyla's maid of honour rushes toward Abi and whisks her into the photographer's next shot, much to the photographer's dismay. Lyla stands frozen like a mannequin, offering her little sister only a tiny wink, and mouths "Are you okay?" The photographer whisks Lyla back outside, leaving Abi with the bustling girls.

Sneaking down the hallway to the dining room's filtered warmth; she runs her hand along the buffet cabinet and finds the familiar gap behind the old wooden table. In her favourite hiding spot, she crouches, ensuring the lacy veil of the crocheted tablecloth is positioned the right way allowing adequate air and a good line of vision. She listens to the sounds of the girls from the distant sunroom and tugs at the tiny silver chain around her neck. Lyla presented it to her this morning; a silver ballet slipper pendant against her skin.

Grandma's voice cuts into the air.

"She's scared about being a flower girl but it's probably more about Lyla leaving. Come on, Earl, that girl's had more change in the last three years than any kid should have to go through. Just let it go. At least for today."

Grandma's shoes click across the floor then stop dead. Chunky heels lie perfectly beneath chubby nylon legs. Grandpa's shiny black shoes slowly follow.

"I'm just saying that after this wedding is over, we need to rethink it all. She's not listening; and she keeps taking off on us. Today of all days. She was half way to the house this time." His voice scrapes the last words like the sandpaper he used to smooth the porch. "One day she'll get there."

"I know, Earl. But it's a big day and Lyla leaving is going to be hard on her. She's been through so much." Grandma's feet turn toward his and Abi holds her breath. She is on the edge of exposure. She imagines their faces together, as close as their toes. She silently sucks in as much air as possible.

He clears his throat. "Well, we can't have her heading over there is all. For one thing it's not safe. But God knows what would happen if she went in there. We need to rethink tearing it down and selling the land."

A gap of silence hangs between his navy pant legs and the flouncy bottom of her mint dress. Abi wonders if they are looking at each other. Are they smiling? Frowning? Their knees give nothing away. She holds her breath and wonders how much longer she can.

"Another day." Grandma finally whispers. "Let's discuss it another day. Let's get Lyla settled in town and then figure things out. And I want to sign Abi up for those ballet lessons she's been asking for. Maybe give her something to focus on. Earl? Earl?"

Grandpa lets out a lingering sigh and Abi sips a bit of air in the wake of the noise.

"Earl, she needs something new to think about. She's been asking since Christmas when she saw that Nutcracker show on TV. That's eight months, Earl. It's not just a phase."

"I just don't see how, Ruth." His voice is barely a whisper. Abi crouches down to better see his body, angling her right eye beneath the scalloped edge of the table cloth. He is running his fingers through his grey hair and staring at Grandma. "Something's got to give. Dr. Whatserface is twice a week now for how long? Is it helping? Driving all the way to town and back and now dancing lessons?"

"Dr. Shipley," Grandma says. "We don't know where we'd be without her do we, so we can't tell how much she's helped her these past three years. I will drive Abi to her ballet lessons. It's not that expensive, Earl."

Grandpa shakes his head. "Easy to say now. What about in the winter? Thirty minutes there and thirty minutes back in the dead of winter so a six-year-old can leap around." He stroked his hair again. "She can leap around here! Ruth, you know I'd do anything for that girl." He pauses. "I just, I just don't know how to do good by her."

"And that house over there, rotting away. We need to tear it down before she wanders over. Tear it down and get some money for the little patch of land at least. Word in town is the high schoolers are comin' and doin' drugs over there, or making like it's some house of horrors."

"I can't think about it today, Earl."

"Well, we're not made of money. Ballet lessons and a psychiatrist and God knows what else she needs when the farm's barely making it and we owe already on this place."

Abi frowns and curls her knees into herself beneath the table.

"I'll pay for them." A whoosh of white satin flows by as Lyla enters the room. "If Abi wants ballet lessons, I will pay for them. I'll even come and get her and drive her there and back."

"Lyla, that's silly. You'll be living in town."

"I don't mind. I'll take her," she says. "Sign her up for when I'm back from my honeymoon. It's time to go. Where's Abi?"

"Probably missing again?" Grandpa groans. "I'll go find her." His feet stride toward the satin skirt and stop. Abi hears him kissing her sister on the cheek before his feet stomp out and she hears him calling her name. She waits a long minute after Lyla and Grandma leave and tugs at the pendant. A moment later, she climbs from beneath the table and re-puffs her dress.

It is time to toss the petals.

Brisé

ABI CREEPS from her bed knowing Grandma is convinced she is asleep. She stands in the quiet light of her nightlight and reaches for the pale, leather ballet slippers Lyla brought her today. They are soft to the touch and smell of newness. She slips them on her feet. They are so light she feels as though she could leap and soar across her bedroom like a bird. She slides silently toward her jewelry box and opens it.

She watches as the plastic ballerina stands still, her arms perfectly arched above her head, her toes pointed. Abi points her own toes, then spins on the hardwood floor as flashes of her wall, window, painting, zoom by over and over until she realizes they are spinning and she has stopped. Nauseated, she turns back to her bed, silently blowing a kiss to the plastic ballerina. Leaving her slippers on, she puts her head on the pillow and closes her eyes struggling to remember the positions and words Lyla taught her today.

She enters Miss Darling's Dance Studio and climbs up the narrow tile staircase to where piano keys plunk the same melody over and over behind a closed wooden door. Three little girls in pale pink tutus stand in a single line waiting for the door to open.

Abi does not join them. Instead she stands next to a slim boy in dark grey tights. A long green T-shirt hangs past his bottom. Noting that his ballet shoes are black while hers are standard soft pink, she stares at the way his feet are placed, heels together, toes in opposite directions.

He raises and lowers his body bending his knees.

"Why are your feet like that?" She asks.

"I'm practising first." His tone is matter of fact.

"Before what?"

"What?" He put his toes back together and leans in toward her. He is considerably taller than Abi, at least a head taller with spiked hair making the difference even more.

"You said you were practising first. First before what?"

"First position, silly!" He shakes his head. "I am doing 'pliees' in ballet first position." He watches her face, uncomprehending.

She nods, thinking back to Lyla talking to her about ballet. The word 'plie' is familiar and Lyla did mention the numbers.

"I guess you wouldn't know," he continues, a little show-offy.

Abi shrugs, fearful that everyone in the class will be better than her. She bends and fiddles with a strand of thread coming out of her tights by her knee, circling it with her finger into a small ball.

The boy spins a twirl on one foot ending unexpectedly off-kilter. He comes to a stop grasping the wall as his face opens into a wide embarrassed smile. "Whoops." He laughs, making light of the fact that he'd misjudged.

Abi extends her chest and points her toe, mimicking his movements. "I'm going to be Clara in the Nutcracker," she states with certainty.

"Oh yeah?"

"Yeah." Was he questioning such a fact? "I saw it on TV at Christmas. Twice!" Are you the only boy here?"

"I think so."

"'Ballerinas are girls." She reaches for her slipper pendant, jumping into her mind's eye and imagining dancing on a stage.

"Well we aren't called ballerinas." He rolls his dark eyes. "But of course we take ballet. Who do you think is lifting the ballerinas, you dodo?"

He was right. She hadn't thought about it. She would need a Nutcracker Prince. She grins her gap-toothed smile. She should have been hurt that he called her dodo, but she kind of liked it.

The piano music stops and she hears a woman's faint voice followed by a scuffle of feet behind the door.

"It's our turn," the boy says. "I'm Rocket. You can stand beside me if you want. I can show you stuff."

Abi, Rocket and the girls enter the room and stand in two rows. The butterflies come but she warns them to stay in check. She stands tall beside Rocket and adjusts her leotard.

From a door beyond the piano a woman appears; the perfect ballerina. Miss Darling is tall and slim and stands as though a rope is holding her head in a perfect line toward the ceiling, Her ballet slippers, rigid like the toes were filled with rocks, wind up to her calves with pink satin ribbons. Her leotard, a soft baby blue, has a V-neck allowing a shiny blue stoned pendant to display a perfect triangle.

"Class, we have a new student today. Please join me in welcoming Abigail." Her voice is clear and her words envelop Abi like a gentle breeze. She steps forward and reaches her arm toward Abi while her leg extends forward with perfect poise. Her golden hair is tied up in a bun, like the ballerina in the poster that hangs on Abi's bedroom wall.

Miss Darling places a gentle hand on Abi's hair and whispers "Welcome" as though Abi is the only student there. Abi stares at her perfect pink nails that seem to dance themselves as she walks toward the front of the class.

Then, there is only Miss Darling. Abi stands in a straight row pointing her toes out and in and out and in. Then, she and Miss Darling prance around the room in 'princess walks' on their tippy toes. Finally, they twirl. Abi is proud. She has remembered all the moves Lyla showed her.

Miss Darling shows a twirl of her own which she calls a 'pirouette'. Abi watches Miss Darling lift her leg and twirl on the tip of her toe like the tiny plastic ballerina that lives in the jewel box. Abi does not want to leave. She wants to watch Miss Darling; to hold her creamy hand and 'princess walk' together, forever.

A low growl rises from behind and instinctively Abi knows it is the wolf. Miss Darling stops spinning and stares at the wolf. He is at the door, lowering his paw, about to pounce. Miss Darling turns back to Abi. Her eyes are pleading. She screams at Abi to run. Abi screams. Her feet won't move. She screams again, louder.

Grandma's arms are wrapped around her like a thick blanket. She rocks Abi until the sobs subside and Grandma gently pulls the slippers from her feet before Abi falls back to sleep.

Mr. Dodds always winks when he hands Abi a fresh strawberry or the shiniest apple from his fruit stand. The stand spans the entire storefront of Dodds' Marketplace where he has personally welcomed the town's residents every day for the past forty years. Today it is cherry season, and he animatedly points to several before selecting the darkest red one and plucking it by the stem.

"For you, my sweet." He hands Abi the cherry and she thanks him, searching back through the glass window for Grandma. She should really have her approval but Grandma is nowhere to be seen. She smiles and pops the cherry into her mouth, remembering to be careful about the pit.

It is Saturday morning, and like every Saturday morning Abi can remember, she and Grandma have driven to town for groceries. Grandma sees it as some sort of mission, fiercely crossing things off her list with the ballpoint pen that seemingly lives behind her ear. Abi doddles behind, working on her letters to read the labels on boxes and cans or, better yet, wandering back to the sidewalk to watch Mr. Dodds greeting everyone.

Like every summer Saturday, the town bustles with tourists and locals. They sit on red metal chairs outside Beans Coffee Emporium sipping from soup bowl cups, or walking from

Brisé

store to store in search of perfect gifts. Abi sits herself down on the rickety bench next to Mr. Dodds.

"Lots of folks out today," he states and Abi wonders why she hears this same thing every Saturday. Is it not obvious? She politely agrees with him. Sitting next to Mr. Dodds has become a tradition she does not want to sever.

She stares into the morning crowd, and watches a clump of teenage girls move as one in a fit of laughter. A tall man talks into his cell phone, oblivious to those around him, a woman pushes a stroller with three other toddlers hanging on to a makeshift rope.

Across the street, her eye catches the smiling face of Rocket. He stands alone, waving fiercely until she waves back. He dashes away into the crowd. She searches with her eyes but cannot find him.

"How are the peaches, is it too early?" The scrawny lady with the long nose and droopy arm flap reaches across the fruit stand to some light-coloured peaches near the back. "Oh, yes, I think so. These needed more time on the tree." She laughs and puts the small peach back, only then catching sight of Abi. "Oh, hello dear." Her voice lowers and Abi notices her eyes turn back up to Mr. Dodds. "How was the wedding?" She looks back at Abi.

"Good." Abi grins, pleased to have a topic to discuss. She describes being a flower girl and throwing the petals. She explains how Lyla and her new husband drove off with tin cans tied to their car. But as her words slide softly off her tongue, she notices the woman is not listening. Perhaps her volume is too low? Perhaps she is mumbling like Grandpa sometimes complains she does. Regardless, the woman has turned to Mr. Dodds as though Abi is not there.

"So nice for them to have something good happen finally." The woman shakes her head. "That Lyla really turned out okay after all. Such a blessing."

"Yes, she did." Grandma appears, loaded with two canvas

sacs over one arm and another, tall paper bag in the other. "Lyla is just fine. And so is Abi. Thank you. Abi, let's go." Grandma motions for Abi to stand up and take one of the bags. They walk away and Abi notices Grandma's stern walk. Abi skulks in shame, a feeling so familiar yet one she does not understand.

Grandma says nothing as the two walk by the coffee shop patio, past Denby's Art Store and into the waft of warm bread and cinnamon effusing from Pearl's Bakeshop. Grandma pauses a moment, staring through the window at a rack of dainty pastries. Abi knows she is debating the expense over the joy it will bring. Abi secretly sends silent messages hoping Grandma will receive them and go inside.

It works.

"Wait here with the bags," Grandma says, putting them down on the small stone wall. "I'll get us some iced tarts and appease Grandpa with one of those apple rolls he likes so much." She snickers at her scheme. "I'll just be a second. Stay here," she warns.

Abi stands a while, then sits herself down on the wall, pleased that it seems her feet are closer to the ground than the last time she did so. Perhaps next year she'll be able to sit with both feet firmly on the sidewalk. Perhaps if she does more stretching in ballet class. She closes her eyes, willing another silent message to Grandma to buy extra iced tarts or maybe something else but her telepathic efforts are thwarted by his voice.

"Miss Abigail." Jay takes a few steps forward from where he's come. "We meet again."

"Hi Jay," she says without hesitation, comforted that Grandma is nearby and many strangers mill about. She watches as the teenage boy plants himself directly in front of her. "How are you?"

"Good." He smiles.

She speaks the words she's been longing to say. "I want to come and see your house."

"Oh, you do, do you?" He raises his eyebrows. "Why is that?"

"Because it's close to my house, I guess. And the kitchen smells of bread, and the little girl's room is pink," she replies, pleased.

He nods. His eyes are dark and droopy, like someone about to fall asleep.

"I want you to come." He whispers and tingles of fear caress the back of her neck beneath her ponytail. She sees him again, not in front of her but inside her mind. His mouth opens like the wolf. She can feel his panting heat. She jolts backward, almost falling off the wall.

"Take care, Miss Abigail." He is Jay again, smiling in his baseball cap. He turns to cross the street and vanishes into the crowd as the bells from Pearl's Bakeshop chime at Grandma's movement through the door.

"We'll have these for dessert after the ham tonight." Grandma says as they walk to the car. She gently pops the pastry box on top of the grocery bags in the trunk. "Now, let me think if there's anything else we need in town." Lost in her thoughts Grandma pulls her list from her pocket while Abi walks around to the car's passenger side and goes inside. Across the small parking lot she stares at the back entrance of Miss Darling's Dance Studio. Miss Darling sits on the staircase and lifts her hand in the air.

———

IT HAS BEEN two weeks since the wedding. Lyla is back. She and her new husband came Friday night to stay the weekend. They arrived with dark with suntans and brought Abi a Spanish doll in red and black lace dress. Abi believes Lyla and her husband are still in bed this early morning but Abi has come to sit on the porch and stare at the brown house. She can hear the whirr of Grandpa's saw from deep inside the shed. Grandma is likely busy with her quilting as she does every Sunday.

Abi scoots her bum down to the next step on the porch, wondering. The brown house can't be much farther than where she'd gone the morning of Lyla's wedding. If she walks at a fast pace she will easily find it. She toys with the wrath of Grandma and Grandpa's disapproval. Grandma will threaten to start locking her inside if she keeps running away. She sits still another moment before deciding it is worth it. She silently scoots again to the bottom step and standing to walk.

Back down the gravel road she runs, this time carried forward by her buoyant running shoes and the ease of her jean shorts and T shirt. Meandering along the road past the tree where Jay had glued himself she continues on, farther than she has ever strayed. At the winding bend she stops for a moment, then proceeds up the small hill.

Tall poplar trees part like curtains at a theatre and before her is a hilly patch of grass. It leads to the closed gate of a long, white fence. She slows her pace, across the lawn to the gatepost where she inserts her fingers into the intricate ironwork. Grandma and Grandpa's stern faces appear in her mind. She has come so far knowing instinctively that each step forward is wrong. Still, she reaches her tiny wrist through one of the holes and it unlatches. The gate swings open with a rusty cry.

The brown house, Jay's house, stands before her. The two windows upstairs and two downstairs along with the door make it appear like a giant face. As she approaches, she sees the window eyes are closed. They are covered with wood slats and the door mouth is boarded shut by a horizontal plank that causes the face to grimace.

There is no sign of Jay. No sign of anyone but a faded blue mailbox. She touches it slowly, and the pale image of a robin on a leaf causes her body to jolt. "*Love to hear the robin go tweet tweet tweet.*" She sings a tune she did not know she knew. She stares at the mailbox a moment longer, confused. It is Miss Darling's voice that is singing the song to her.

Approaching slowly, she reaches the front steps and lifts her leg to ascend. Taking hold of the chipped wooden railing, she cries out as a sliver of wood enters her palm. Despite the pain, she carries on up the stairs to the picture window on the left of the door. Its wooden plank lays abandoned on the porch in a cascade of shattered glass. Jagged triangles hang from the window. She slips through the slot wide enough for her small body.

INTO JAY's sitting room Abi tumbles, landing on her knees next to a coffee table covered in dusty, ash filled beer bottles. Glass tubes like straws are strewn on filthy dishes. Cigarette butts dot the brown carpet and a dank stench enters her nostrils. A small strip of sunlight cuts through the broken window causing particles to dance in the air. She slips in to crouch beside an armchair and her pounding heart stops at a crash, then a low thunk.

"Jay?" She knows she should slip back out the way she came and run, with all her might, back home.

Thunk. Closer now, in the dim room where the only other sound is her breath.

"Jay?"

She counts to ten, then ten again. How long can she stay crouched down here? She should creep back across the carpet and out the window and run. RUN. One, two, three, GO! She springs to her feet as a stray cat appears in front of her, squealing and leaping to the windowsill. Abi falls back, her screams melt into gut-wrenching sobs of terror. Surely this isn't Jay's house. It's so dark and smelly. She'd made a terrible mistake. She has to go home, to Grandma's kitchen. It's her turn to set the table.

Lyla runs along the grassy side of the gravel road to gain speed, yelling Abi's name every few seconds. Just moments earlier she'd found Grandma crying and arguing with Grandpa. Abi has run away to the old house again. Despite Lyla's own revulsion at returning to her former home, she's headed out to find her sister.

Now, her own memories of the trail flood back. Good and bad emotions fold into each other like blending batter. She recalls the joy of childhood walks through brown-eyed Susan's to visit Grandma and Grandpa. But soon those memories are blanketed by darkness and evil that occurred that night, three years ago. She approaches the hill she's crested a thousand times before that night, but never since.

Each breath becomes more regular, and Abi finds the courage to pull herself up by the arm of the chair. Adjusting her eyes, she peers toward the arch shaped doorway that leads to a hall. The cat glares and leaps out the window. Abi knows she should too. Instead, she musters the courage to walk forward to the staircase. Sunlight shines from above, illuminating the carpet enough that she can ascend.

Following her instincts, she ignores the first set of double doors and walks down the hallway. She places her hand on a white doorknob, turns it silently and steps inside a small room. A gap in the window board provides enough light to see a bed against the wall. She steps forward, running her index finger along the bedspread. Beside the bed, atop a metal desk, is a trophy with a statue of a baseball player, a stack of books and a three-ring notebook. Abi lifts the notebook and looks at the letters printed neatly on the lines. Sounding them out she says aloud, "J j j a a yy ssssss on! Jason." She falls back on the bed, paralyzed, and digs her fingernails into the bedspread.

NAUSEA OVERTAKES LYLA as she approaches the porch. Pain cuts into her forehead and she leans forward to gag as the memories continue to invade.

She was with her girlfriends at the movies, something with Bradley Cooper. She remembers the smell of the popcorn. Her girlfriend was upset. Her latest love had dumped her. Lyla decided to stay longer so they could talk. It was after midnight when Lyla arrived home that night to the devil red flashing lights. Grandma sat on the porch while someone tied yellow crime tape across the railing. It was as though they were sealing her inside.

Lyla calls out for Abi but hears no response. She smashes the glass and crawls through the broken window into the living room of her former home. In three years, the room she'd known and loved has turned into a crack den. Instinctively, she ascends the stairs and pauses at what used to be her parent's bedroom door. Opening it, she is overwhelmed by the salty scent of blood that lingers in her imagination.

"It's all of them." Grandma words had been so broken Lyla'd taken a while to comprehend. "Your mother the boys. And little Abi's been taken to the hospital. Somehow, she's survived!" Grandma fell into Lyla's chest and sobbed as the reality of the nightmare swelled.

Grandpa had appeared in the doorway, his expression a frozen fossil of fear, his chest covered in so much blood that Lyla could only imagine it belonged to everyone.

Tears roll down Abi's cheeks. She can hear Dr. Shipley's instructions about handling feelings and how Abi should talk about anything she doesn't understand. Frantically she leaves the room and goes to the next one down the hall, finding herself staring at two posters above another small bed. The first poster is planets, spinning in their orbits around the sun. The second shows a white rocket, fire burning below its belly. On the low end table next to the bed, Rocket smiles inside a picture frame. He is grinning ear-to-ear next to a man in a spacesuit. Above their heads are letters: N A S A. Abi began to say them aloud as her sister flies into the room.

"Abi, oh Abi, you scared us. Are you okay?" Lyla sweeps her up and onto the bed. "What are you thinking coming here?"

Talk about anything, Dr. Shipley said. "I came to see Jay," she explains.

"Jay, who is Jay? You mean Jason?"

"He wears a baseball cap"

"Jason? Yes he ... did. You remember Jason, right Abi?" Lyla reaches for her forehead like she is in pain.

Abi shrugs.

"You know Jason was your big brother. We've looked at photos."

"Yes."

"Do you ... do you remember him?"

Abi shrugs again.

"He was 14 when, when he died. You were only three."

Abi nods. Dr. Shipley had explained it as best she could. Grandma and Grandpa too, back, before their words were muted. She looks around the room, trembling. "And Rocket."

"Rocket?"

"Rocket." Abi extends her arm to point at the picture frame.

"That's Ethan." Lyla strokes her little sister's back. "Ethan was our other brother. He was seven, almost the age you are now."

"Rocket." Abi sobs.

"Yes, he liked rockets, spaceships, anything about space. That's him when we went to the Space Center in Florida. You were only," she pauses, "a baby then." Lyla's voice trails off and Abi reaches back to offer a hug.

The two sisters sit in silence rippled only by their melodic cries and sniffles.

"Did you know this was our house?"

Abi shakes her head. "This is Jay's house."

Lyla frowns.

"We need to get out of here. Grandma and Grandpa are frantic, and it's not safe." Lyla continues.

"Come on, let's go back outside." She leads her little sister back down the stairs. They climb back out the window hole. Abi reaches for the mailbox, this time seeing it from the other side.

"Tweet, tweet, tweet," she whispers as Lyla kneels down to wrap her arms around her. "What sweetie?"

"Tweet, tweet, tweet, rockin' robin," Abi whispers.

"Mom used to sing that when she picked up the mail." Lyla sobs, looking up toward the road.

"What does that say?" Abi points to the printing on the other side of the mailbox.

"Our Mommy and Daddy's names" Lyla replies. "Darlene and Martin Scott."

"Darling." Abi smiles and sits on the step. "Like the ballet school."

"Darlene. But yes, her name is like Miss Darling's, where you'll be starting your lessons soon."

The two sit in silence as Abi imagines the beautiful lady from the ballet studio from her dreams.

"Abi, do you remember the other parts?" Lyla's voice cracks. "About Daddy?"

Abi stares back toward her grandparents' home before rising and turning back to the window. Jay stands before her in the darkness of the living room. He is the wolf again. He lunges forward through the glass. The fur around his mouth is covered in blood.

She steps back.

"I didn't mean it," Jay's voice is strong. His jaw clenches as he reaches for her arm. He is the boy again but he holds a bloodied knife.

She struggles to let go.

"Abi, what are you doing? "Abi can hear Lyla's voice in the distance, like someone trying to infiltrate a dream. Abi screams as Jay grabs her other wrist.

"Abi, I couldn't do it. Not to you." His eyes are yellow, without expression. "I didn't know what I was doing!"

Abi breaks free and turns to run, crashing into Lyla as Jay's voice groans from somewhere in the distance, then disappears into silence.

"Abi, what is it?" Lyla holds her tight. "What are you seeing?"

"They said Daddy killed them." Abi speaks, trancelike. "But he didn't."

"What?"

"Jason killed them." Abi whispered. "It was Jason. He tried to kill me too."

ABI CAN SEE Grandma and Grandpa approaching but they don't see her nor Lyla behind the shade of the oak tree. Abi can hear Grandma though. She is speaking to Grandpa in low tones. "It's time she understands it all. Oh Earl, did we do the right thing?"

Stern, Grandpa stops walking. He takes Grandma's arm firmly. "We did what we had to do."

"But Earl, maybe it's time to tell the truth." Grandma looks up.

"Nothing more to tell. Our baby girl married that low-life loser and we had to protect our grandson's name. He's our blood. People around here with their talk. It's better this way." Grandpa lets go of her arm as they continue approaching. His expression softens as he sees Abi and Lyla.

"But Earl. I don't know how much longer I can live with myself." Grandma cries out then sees her granddaughters on the porch. Her face is red and she pulls her fist in to her chest and turns to Lyla. "Is she okay?" Grandma collapses onto the steps pulling Abi toward her.

"She's okay." Lyla rocks Abi in her arms. "Everything is going to be okay."

Lyla stands to face her grandfather eye to eye. "But, she remembers more than we give her credit for."

About K. Bradley

K. Bradley (Kathi Nidd)'s debut mystery novel, Snowdrifts was published in 2016 and she is currently working toward the publication of two additional mystery thrillers set in the same fictional city.

Her poetry has appeared in publications by The Poetry Institute of Canada, Polar Expressions Publishing, Haunted Waters Press and Quills Magazine. She also has several stories published in CommuterLit e-magazine. A former member of The Ottawa Story Spinners, Bradley's work appears in five volumes of "The Black Lake Chronicles" short story anthologies.

As the creator of "Fuzzball's Christmas Eve Adventure" Bradley engages adults and children alike while fundraising for animal charities. A student of creative writing, her ultimate goal is to mentor upcoming writers as a creative writing coach.

With a career in pharmacy and healthcare informatics, Bradley pulls from the human side of medicine to provide a unique lens into strong and realistic characters.

Bradley grew up and continues to reside in Ottawa alongside her loving spouse, a spirited mini schnauzer, and a pensive pug.

Read more at www.writingspot.ca or contact Kathi at askthewritingspot@gmail.ca.

Tommy Gun

David Devine

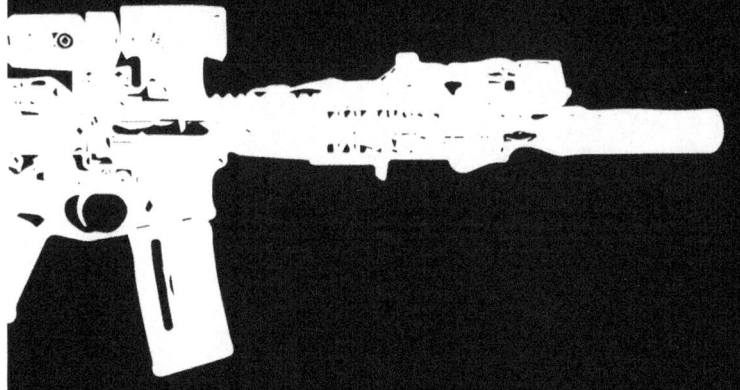

You give them clear instructions at gunpoint, and they do the opposite. It's a death sentence written by their own actions. They have no one to blame but themselves.

Tommy Gun

David Devine

'Scorpio' was the last thing I heard before putting a bullet through the back of his head.

The rain was dense that morning. The creak of the floorboards and the smell of rusted pipes never failed to greet me. They were subtle reminders of my failures.

The bathroom was always a place of meditation. I found peace studying the flowing water from the tap. It was the only time I could escape the haunting problems life gave me.

Working for SWAT wasn't the greatest money, but it was steady money. There were too many things to take care of, and Tommy was less than a perfect brother. Mom was proud of my job; maybe she knew it would piss off Dad. He had no respect for the law. Tommy took after him like most firstborns do. *He* felt it was his job to carry on his old man's legacy. *I* felt it was my duty to make up for his evil.

With Dad locked up and Mom falling ill, everything fell on me. Why shouldn't it? Isn't that how the world works? Everyone looks for a crutch, a scapegoat. My old man is no different. We've both ended lives; the only difference between us is that I don't pick who I kill.

You give them clear instructions at gunpoint, and they do

the opposite. It's a death sentence written by their own actions. They have no one to blame but themselves.

The more I saw suffering, the more I could feel my grit building. It helped with the job, which is good for the family. Whatever's left of it.

A cold cup of instant coffee was all I needed. I hated that aroma just as much as I hated looking at overdue bills. Pushing them aside revealed a new evil. Pictures of healthy people are not what you want to see on a wellness pamphlet that ends with a hefty price. The doctors are no help. There's a reason they pocket their hands when delivering bad news. They know treatments only exist for the rich. Who buys cancer insurance anyways? I could barely afford to keep the lights on.

I can't imagine what Mom would look like right now without me by her side. The poor woman had suffered enough. Clutching her blanket with frigid fingers as if hanging from a cliff. What a terrible way to die. Slowly seeing bits of your soul drift away like ashes from a flame.

I think the stress of the job might finally be getting to me. I haven't been so sure of anything lately. It was like a growing fog in my brain. Sinking my hours into the shooting range was the only thing that made sense. I wouldn't let them take me off rotation that easily, even if I wasn't feeling myself. Besides, being honest with a therapist is the dumbest thing you can do.

I called Tommy again before I left for work. No answer. Three days now, he's been gone. He likes to throw a fit and disappear for a long time. Yelling about how he'd get the money to pay for Mom's meds was not what I wanted to hear from him. I needed him home. I had an upcoming training camp for a few days, and I couldn't leave Mom alone for that long.

I waved to the neighbor on my way to the car. No one on the street knew what I did. I kept things vague, even with Tommy. He kept his fair share of secrets too. He knew if I caught him shooting up that crap, I'd slap him. But I know he cares; about Mom anyways. He just had a tough time showing it. Hopefully, he would come home soon before getting into trouble he couldn't get out of.

The silent drive to the base was another opportunity for meditation. The rain stopped when I pulled up to the security gate. A badge flip and a cold stare always got the metal doors moving. I could feel something was off. Maybe my sixth sense was trying to tell me something.

Getting out of my civilian car was the most normal part of the job. Flashing my badge to two more checkpoints reminded me of where I was. A fortress. We weren't keeping things out. We were keeping things in.

I always stopped to look at the wanted board. Somehow all the criminals looked the same. It was their eyes. They all had the same creature staring through the windows of their dark soul.

What causes someone to abandon all sense of morality? Was it desperation? Hardships? It can't be. Life is tough for everyone. It rains the same on the just and the unjust. All we can do is choose how to react to getting punched in the face. If they die, it's their choice, not mine. I'm okay with that.

The meeting rooms were always dim as if we were keeping secrets from each other. The squad was already drinking the drip coffee and stuffing discount muffins in their face. I'm not a fan. I just need to focus on my job. The faster I move up, the more money I could make. You don't apply for positions here; you volunteer and hope to be compensated later. I guess doing the right thing for the wrong reasons is still doing the right thing.

Trying to find truth in the new equipment manual was interrupted by the blast of a code-silver alarm. Sirens controlled me like a dancing puppet. I sprinted to my locker before my imagination was able to catch up. With no time to think, you had to rely on your reactions.

Like a bear tearing a tree apart, I grabbed my equipment from my locker. I could feel my concentration rising as the sirens beat against my ears like a drum. The longer we took to gear up, the longer lives could be in jeopardy.

This wasn't my first code-silver. I put a few away scumbags in Albany, but this was different. This one was alone and had already shot a hostage.

Sarge reported the latest intel as the SWAT car broke every speed limit in the city. His voice always sounded like he was about to pop a vein. I tightened the grip on my assault rifle as if it were anchoring me to reality.

The SWAT car shifted and took a sharp turn onto the scene. This was it. Go time. The rear doors burst open. The sound of combat boots beat against the pavement. I scanned the site while pressing forward. Damn, bookies loved to keep their windows dirty. We had to go in. Snipers with no visibility were as useless as shooting at the sun.

Sarge took over the negotiations; he always had a way with words; maybe that's why he's been married for over thirty years.

The maintenance crew in the back had already set up an ingress. Industrial ducts suspended by steel cables every two feet were my ticket in. Radio check, gun check, and a boost to the ventilation shaft put me into a dark silver tunnel. My overtraining and lack of nutrition made me the ideal candidate for confined spaces.

I felt like a mouse in a maze, crawling through a science experiment. Moving with an assault rifle while making minimal noise proved to be the biggest challenge. I stopped for a second to slow my heart rate, the fear of the shooter hearing the vents move would paralyze any man. Thin steel walls did their best to guard my life, and my mild claustrophobia wasn't helping.

I spotted the back of his head through a ceiling vent and double-tapped my radio to signal I was in position.

Tommy Gun

Caucasian male, six foot four, black jacket, and a Bugs-Bunny mask. This guy had definitely watched too many movies.

Sarge tried reasoning with him, but the suspect just pressed another hostage to the window at gunpoint. If only he knew shooting another hostage would rain down hellfire.

I got a good visual of the weapon. 357 Magnum, good choice. I had the same one at home.

He shouted at the cops to leave as if haunted, the gun shaking in his hand.

He threw the hostage to the floor and started pacing, occasionally grabbing his head. I lost visual but quickly gained it back. Sweat dripping from under his mask. He's gone too far, and now he knows there's no way out. Perhaps the first hostage killing was a mistake.

His muffled demands fell on deaf ears. He reiterated that they were the ones that made him do this. Something my old man would often say. Blaming others for his transgressions. The only thing you can control is your own damn actions.

His voice carried too much uncertainty as if he was crying. Tommy was always sulking like this. Damned 30-year-old man crying.

The suspect started counting down from three. Ultimatums are never good. My finger tightened around the trigger against my will. My heart started to race. The more he spoke, the more I sweated. I just needed more time to take in the situation. I wished he would stand down. For once, I just wished they would listen.

'Scorpio' was the last thing I heard before putting a bullet through the back of his head. The trigger word. The Sergeant's command that controlled my finger.

I didn't feel anything after the recoil. The world shut off. All I could see was the Bugs-Bunny mask flying into the air.

In all my years on the job, I've never seen a body drop so slowly.

About David Devine

David Devine is an author and screenwriter. He is a first-generation Ukrainian born in Haifa, Israel, and now lives in Ottawa, Canada.
    The series, Galtronia, takes place in the year 2122. The nations of Earth unite under the UN flag to fight off an aggressive alien race from another Galaxy. Vizer and his crew escape the battle only to discover that they are not alone. The Quanrus, a hidden humanoid-frog race, harbor the humans on their planet and share their technology that's too dangerous for them to use. Learning about Earth's destruction, the last humans work with their new allies to build the most formidable force in the universe. With human bravery and Quanrus technology, they seek to destroy a secret weapon the Galtronians have brought to their doorstep.

    GALTRONIA TRILOGY:
    Book1: Water Valley (Forthcoming)
    Book2: Heart of Pulcore (Forthcoming)
    Book3: Dreads of Destiny (Forthcoming)

OTHER DEVINE NOVELS:
    The Heart Locker (2020)

The Heart Locker is Devine's first published novel that follows the life of Claire as she goes through a divorce only to have her life changed for the better before the problems of her past try to seep back in.

Find me on Amazon

Voices in the Void

Matt C. Sully

When Singh 12-b is struck by an unknown disaster, Starseed engineers Graham and Park are isolated from family and crew, desperate to survive, and terrified to discover the truth behind the planet's destruction.

Voices in the Void

Matt C. Sully

During his twenty years as a Starseed engineer, Graham had learned one immutable fact: Flashing lights meant bad news.

The domed cap of Singh Tower was a metallic pimple on the vibrant and stark expanse of planet Singh 12-b. Inside, two engineers converged on a boiling kettle in the minuscule kitchenette. Graham prepped the tea bags when Park's watch chimed and flickered.

"Station's coming 'round now," he said.

Graham nodded. "I'll bring yours over."

Park tucked himself into the bolted seat, awakening his handheld in case the boss wanted to talk numbers. He flipped a switch on the sloped controls, opening a channel for the expected broadcast. Static crackled and vibrated the console speaker, an auditory fog through which ghostly voices often hailed.

Graham set a steaming mug in front of his colleague. "Light chatter today."

Trapped transmission waves bounced previous conversations between the planet and its dense, nearly opaque atmosphere. Park often heard his own words returned like echoes of history, reports he'd given from hours or even days before. Today was relatively quiet.

"Good," said Park. "I hate the sound of my voice."

Graham seated himself nearby, a cubbyhole filled with broken Starseed components and scrap ambitiously welded into malformed chairs. A plaque bolted to the wall said 'Lounge,' letters torched along its metal face.

The pops and hisses fell silent and Park began a brief and well-rehearsed exchange with the operations director. Graham sipped his tea, staring at the curved ceiling as if envisioning the station orbiting above. With numbers confirmed and half-hearted praise given, the director was prepared to sign off. Then Park requested personal comms with Samantha Bloomberg.

A tea bag struck the back of Park's head with a wet smack.

"She doesn't want to talk to me," Graham said.

Park dampened the white noise with the twist of a knob and leaned over the back of his seat.

"Look. Everyone's coming down in a week and I'm not letting you two do that passive sidestep nonsense. You two argue, then avoid each other until someone breaks."

"That's our speed of conflict resolution."

"It's silly. The sooner you talk, the sooner it's resolved."

"Wouldn't *you* rather talk to her?" asked Graham. "Convince her what a shlub she married and how she should run away with you to Titan?"

"Titan folk are strange at best. Besides, I've been saving for my own ship, and if I'm going to steal your wife, it's gonna be in style."

"Glad she'll be well looked after, but this isn't a new argument, and it's no big deal. Really."

"I'm not trying to save your marriage, Graham. Let's make a list."

"Ugh," said Graham. "Not a list."

Park tapped his extended index finger. "One. We're a team

that needs to work together, efficiently. Two." His middle finger joined the session with vigor. "The colonists are always a bit skittish when they first land. Some are excited. Some are freaked out. We don't need tower crew bringing any awkward vibes to an already emotionally-heightened situation." Park's hand formed a 'W.' "Three. Sam is a culinary wizard and I'm tired of eating MREs."

"I can cook."

Park chuckled. "You cannot. Now get over here and talk with your wife before the station moves out of range."

Park picked up the used tea bag from the floor and dismissed himself. The static was gone, but no one spoke.

Graham pressed the button on the mic. "Samantha?"

"How are my plants?" she asked.

"Growing nicely. You've seen the data."

"That's data. I can't actually *see* the plants. Any sign of rot or mold? The moisture levels in there are concerning."

"It's fine. They look good, really. They're taking on the color of the soil like you thought."

"I can't wait to see."

"Sam." Graham took a breath. "I know you're upset with me...."

"I'm tired of having the same conversation, Graham."

"I know."

"You said Austin would be our last colony commencement. Here we are about to start with Singh and you've already been talking about the next one. Park is packing up after this. Why can't you?"

"Starseed's age cutoff is 50; Park *has* to go."

"We talked about making a home somewhere Graham. Setting down roots. We can't do that if we keep moving every few years."

"We can make a home on the next colony or go back to the Gliese system."

"I don't want to go back to Gliese."

"Mars then. We were good there."

"That was a long time ago, and Mars isn't what it used to be. Too many slums."

Graham looked over at Park to see if he was listening. The stout engineer was scrubbing dishes, a short task considering they used the same utensils for every meal.

"It's like this damned station," Sam continued. "Everything up here is old, used, way past its prime."

"It's fine, Sam."

"You said yourself there's parts here that needed replacing five years ago and still haven't been serviced. Starseed isn't living up to its end. We shouldn't be renewing contracts with a company that doesn't care about its people."

"Careful, Sam. This isn't a private channel."

"Like they're paying anyone to listen in. I don't—" A faint voice greeted Samantha in the background. She answered back. "Hey, sweetie."

"Is that Mina?" asked Graham. "Shouldn't she be in school?"

"Her class is doing work study now."

"And she's working with you in the lab?"

"Yeah."

"Not engineering?"

Sam sighed. "She has other interests, Graham. Besides, she's got high marks in engineering. You saw to that. She doesn't need to study what she already knows."

"Okay. I get it."

Graham let his finger off the button for a moment. Park's voice came in across the static, words as clear as they were yesterday: "Storms brewing in the valley, but otherwise all is well, Station."

"Look." Graham interrupted Park's time-bending broadcast. He leaned closer to the mic, his lips on the metal grating. "If this needs to be our last contract, then it will be. We can stay here and actually see it through with the colonists. Or we start fresh once other companies begin to settle in."

"What? With one of the mining groups?"

"Or community builders. They'll need engineers with local knowledge and experience. We'll figure it out."

"I really hope that's true."

"It is. It will be."

The quiet was long. Finally, she responded. "I do miss you."

"I miss you too," he said.

"Do you wanna talk with Mina?"

"Yes. Of course."

"Hang on."

Park's rerun exchange with Starseed's orbiting Station was over. Buzzes and whines controlled the open airwaves while Samantha fetched their daughter.

"Hey, Dad."

"Mina," said Graham. "I have something very serious to tell you."

"Is it about you and Mom?"

"Yes. In a way."

"Um, okay."

"Are you listening?"

"Yes."

Graham took a breath. "Plants are gross and dumb."

"Dad!"

"It's true. And you can't get diseases from machines."

"You're ridiculous. I *like* botany."

"But us engineers are way snappier."

Park shouted from the far kitchenette. "It's true!"

Mina giggled. "That's not how you say it, and if you and Mister Chen are the examples for what's snap, then I'm keeping my focus on botany."

Graham laughed. "Well, it's your life, but engineers make the world go 'round. That's all I'm saying."

"I think that's actually angular momentum, but sure."

"Okay, you big geek. How's school going?"

Static.

Graham toyed with the mic button. "Mina?"

The radio speaker was an undulating sea of warbles and pops. She was gone.

Park joined him at the console, checking the signal readout and tapping his watch.

"Out of range," he said. "Sorry. They'll come back 'round in three hours. We may be able to pick up the signal then."

"That's alright." Graham toggled the switch, silencing the spectral frequencies. "It ended on a relative high note with Sam."

"Told you it would work out. Watch out for those builders though. TZ and Corona are essentially mob fronts. You get involved with those guys, you end up with a horse head in your sheets."

"Is there any part of the conversation you *didn't* hear?"

"Whatever I missed will bounce back around anyway." Park smiled. "There's no secrets on Singh 12-b."

"I'm sorry about Sam. She didn't mean anything by what she said."

"About the slums? I don't care about that."

"She's right about Starseed though. The station, the panels, these bolts that keep stripping. They're not running the same business they were when we started. It's a coin and credit operation now."

"Starseed's cheap," said Park, eying the console to be certain the radio was off, "but they've stuck with us for quite a while. If I wasn't being forced out, I'd give them twenty more years."

"That kind of loyalty is unheard of anymore, Park."

"I'm a Starseed engineer, a really good one too. I've got years left, Graham."

"Hey. You're a bad-ass engineer, the best, but this is it,

Park. The last hurrah. If you don't want to spend your twilight years as a shuttle driver, you need to start seriously working on what you're going to do next."

"That's the thing." Park looked toward a light pulsating on a far console. "I don't want to do anything else."

Graham followed his colleague's gaze. "What is it?"

"Weather warning. Come on."

The men crossed the lines of readouts and screens, each showcasing data in neat bars and columned numbers. Rows of switches and plastic-domed bulbs filled the stations, empty chairs waiting for crew to be assigned to their post. Everything indicated order and readiness, a multi-faceted machine primed to conquer the planet just outside, except something was wrong. Lights were flashing.

"I've never seen that," said Graham. "What's it mean?"

"There's..." Park squinted, mouthing something before starting again. "There's an atmospheric disturbance. *Several* disturbances."

"What kind of disturbances?"

Another nearby light began to blink and a digital needle shuddered in its tiny hemisphere.

"Well, shit," said Graham. "The seismograph's twitching, Park. What's happening out there?"

"According to this, multiple celestial objects have breached the atmosphere and made impact with the planet."

"Uhhhhhh."

"Graham." The middle-aged engineer turned to his colleague, hands raised like a surrendering soldier. "Don't panic, but we're about to be struck by several shockwaves which may destroy this facility."

"What do we do?"

"We get moving. We get moving, very fucking fast."

AN ARRAY of crimson-lit consoles vied for the men's attention. The same shrill alarm screamed through every speaker. The cap walls began to rattle.

"Do we need this?" shouted Graham, a knot of cable aloft in his sweaty fist.

Park didn't respond. He was digging through the 'Lounge' pile like a dog in a graveyard. The hideous chairs had been toppled, scraps of wire and shaped metal strewn across the cap floor. A deep rumble echoed through the domed structure, burrowing into the men's ears.

Graham slid a bin of console components over to Park, dodging his blind throws.

He shouted again. "Do we need this?"

Park turned, pausing on the junk-drawer equivalent below Graham's panicked face.

"No!" yelled Park. "Grab your tools and our suits!"

The elevator door was propped open. Park tossed in an armful of scraps and checked his watch. They had exhausted three minutes, neither knowing just how long it would be before the first shockwave struck.

The resonant bass rose to a roar. Interior panels rippled, the seams between them parting and closing like mouths gasping for air. Something snapped behind the walls.

Graham rushed past with the suits. "That sounded important!"

Park hustled to the radio console and flipped the bolt covers, setting his electric spanner to work. Graham lifted Park's helmet from the console and tossed the heavy uniforms into the elevator atop the ruin of technology.

"Send it down!" shrieked Park, down-turned thumb jabbing the air while his other hand loosened the final bolt.

Graham nodded. He kicked away the pipe blocking the doors and slapped the 'down' button.

As the elevator descended into the tower beneath, a series of tinks sounded all around them, bullets deflecting off an

Voices in the Void

armored car. What followed was a horrific howl that shook the world.

"How do *we* get down?" screamed Graham, inches from Park's face.

Park hefted the detached radio and mic to a circular outline in the floor, pounding the shape with his foot.

"Open this hatch!"

Graham knelt. Beneath the protective cover was a single red button. He slammed it with his palm. Stored pressure hissed in reaction and the hatch opened a few centimeters. Graham helped it the rest of the way and dropped himself into the hole.

The alarms, no longer audible in the cap, were deafening within the buried walls of the tower. Above them, stripped and severed bolts fired in all directions, their liberated panels falling to the ground. Graham held his arms high.

"Come on!"

Park unloaded the heavy radio. He bent his knees and readied to leap down when something large crashed into the cap.

Something flew into the hatch and the artificial lights of the cap blinked out. Graham was thrown to the ground, screaming with fear. The blast was like nothing he'd ever experienced. It was crushing. His bones ached. His organs tightened and his ears bled.

The walkway beneath him rose and fell in waves. It was as if a foreign entity had latched onto him, shaking the life from his body. He stopped screaming long enough to open his eyes, and there was Park. The Starseed engineer had fallen onto him from above.

"Dammit! I thought the whole cap had crashed onto me!"

Graham's shouts were like pebbles gyrating in his throat, but they made no sound. Park mouthed something too, immediately realizing the futility. The first blast had come and gone, but the horrific noises continued unabated. Neither man could hear beyond the destructive cacophony, and more shockwaves traveled in the first one's wake. They came to finish what it started.

Metallic shrieks called to the engineers as new sections of the cap tore free. Bolted interior groaned with resistance against the relentless forces, sending a violent vibrato through Graham's skull.

Park removed himself from his smothered partner and mimed new instructions. He pointed above them, then to the far ends of the passageway. The lights of the tower flickered. Park's gestures in the electric strobes reduced him to slow motion, yet Graham nodded with comprehension.

Though named 'Singh Tower,' Starseed's colonist facility was almost entirely below the planet's surface. It was essentially a giant screw, literally drilled into the layers of soil and rock, then detached and capped with a dome housing. They were two parts, the tower and the cap, and Graham knew what Park knew. The cap was already destroyed, but its locks into the tower threatened to shred the dividing seal between them. They had to let it go.

At each end of the tower's wide expanse was an emergency release, appropriately contained within a bright red box. Graham moved to the box at his end. Park lumbered to its duplicate on the hallway's opposite side. A new wave, meanwhile, seemed to come from everywhere.

The grated path shimmied beneath the men's booted feet. They struggled to remain upright as the room threatened to knock them flat. Fine dust swirled in Graham's face, dust that could only have come from outside. The ventilation fans were losing the fight and the acrid odor of freshly-churned Singh moved through his nostrils. He could taste it, raw and bitter.

Gripping the sides of his box, Graham read the affixed sign: 'CAP RELEASE. FOR EMERGENCIES ONLY.'

The instructions on the box were simple. Pull the lever, press the button, but each man needed to release their half of the cap at the same instant. If their timing failed, they'd get exactly what they'd hoped to avoid. With one part free and the other held in place, the cap would become a crowbar, prying open the roof of the tower.

Graham put both hands on his lever and pulled. He could see Park in the shifting dark doing the same, but the distance was too great and too clouded to witness a countdown, and he certainly couldn't hear the man. Graham would need to listen for the hollow drum of Park's locks sliding out of their hold. He reached for his button, waiting for his cue, when a third shockwave pummeled what remained of the battered dome. The tower around them echoed the blast and the walkway rose and fell like a rogue tidal wave.

Graham was thrown to the floor again, knocking his head. As the ground rumbled and the low sky decimated the planet's surface, the walls of the tower bulged. Singh 12-b threatened to crush the entire structure. Graham looked up from the floor, wiping blood from his head. He peered into the winking dark.

Park's red box still clung to the wall, but rock and aluminum beams had formed a sloppy cone of rubble where Park once stood. Graham steadied himself, taking measured steps toward the mound of spilled planet and broken metal. Halfway across the shaky platform, he spotted Park beneath the debris. The engineer was bruised, bleeding and buried from the waist down. One of his arms was limp. The other was waving Graham back.

The tower ceiling trembled, jumping like the lid on a boiling pot. The cap was ripping it loose. If the windy assault continued, the tower would be torn open, the Starseed crew pulled up into the heart of the storm. There was no time to dig him out.

Graham ran. He ran back to his side of the tower, his path a funhouse floor. He didn't know how Park would activate his cap release. He hoped he could. He knew he had to.

Park snatched loose rocks within reach and tossed them at the button. With every throw, the pile over him shifted, sending a slow avalanche closer to his head and covering more of the box.

The first rock was too high. The pile compressed Park's ribs. The bottom of the box was now concealed too, centimeters below his target.

Graham reached his position, hand stalled against the button. He closed his eyes, waiting for the signal when Park's side was free. In the dark of his mind he thought of death. He thought of pain and the invasive nature of his employer. He thought of the role he played in conquering new worlds and if he was a villain in each planet's story or the bearer of promise. He wondered if this tower would be his tomb. Then he thought of Samantha and Mina. He thought of his family, and the fear subsided.

Park took a labored breath and threw again. The projectile landed too low, dropping through the floor. The rock mound slid, forcing his neck askew. Only the top of the button was left visible.

His lungs worked in shallow pumps. Black spots were beginning to dominate his view. Relying on his final throw to save them would be foolish. Rather than lifting another rock, Park examined the structure of the mess atop him. A beam wedged into the grating of the floor held much of it in place. If he could remove it, the mountain of foreign stone and soil would spill out, colliding with the box and the button inside.

He thought of his mother's gentle face, his father's weathered hands. He thought of Mars. Park balled his hand into a fist and pounded the beam until it gave way.

Everything shook and rattled, and within the chaos Graham heard what he'd been waiting for. He leaned into his button. A multitude of thunks encircled him as the cap locks released, and the environment abruptly changed. The room calmed. Lights steadied and brightened. The unnatural storm continued to move overhead, but the roof of the tower had settled.

"Park!"

Graham called to his partner as he ran, his voice audible once more. He shouted as he sprinted to the rock slide. He shouted as he cleared the debris. He shouted as he pounded Park's chest and the engineer coughed his way back to existence.

When he knew Park was alive, Graham collapsed by his side.

Park checked his watch, and held out a finger.

"Okay," he said. "Let's make a list."

Park's list was exhaustive, well beyond his ten-finger visual aid. The men replaced broken equipment, soldered torn wiring, and welded together panels to shore up the compromised tower walls. Floor by floor they inspected the storage area, the vehicle bay, water reservoir, filtration hub, lower control center, kitchen, mess hall, fitness room, sun room, living quarters, and the bulk of the facility, the labs. There wasn't time to bring it back to pristine condition, but the tower would hold.

Park, arm bound in a sling, completed everything one-handed, though he struggled to get into his suit.

"Bad-ass engineer need some help?" asked Graham.

Park zipped up the work suit, an EMU modified for leaner mobility and with a lot more pockets. A reflective blue 'S' shone across the back. With his injured arm tucked within, the sleeve dangled flaccid at Park's side. He thrust his helmet at Graham.

"Just help me put this on, and connect my oxygen. We missed Station's last loop around, but I want this radio tower up before nightfall," said Park. "Without comms, they won't know what happened."

"*We* still don't know what happened."

"That's the other thing. If the air or the ground is too compromised, we have to tell them to stay off-planet."

"Forever?"

With Park's helmet affixed, their conversation continued through small mics and earpieces.

"Until it's safe," said Park. "Let's not worry until there's something to worry about. Alright?"

Graham nodded and Park pressed the overhead button. The hissing eruption signaled the door's mechanics were working, yet the hatch did not open. Something was blocking their exit.

Brute force moved the hatch a millimeter or two at best and, though the elevator could no longer rise to cap level, its hydraulic system could be repurposed to push nearly anything out of their way. With a tripod of support beams bolted onto a hollow shaft, a fitted pipe was thrust upward into the hatch door. The world was theirs again. They just had to see what was left of it.

Topside, a dust cloud swirled to every horizon. The shadows and shapes moving within were indiscernible from one another. With the naturally purple haze of the planet, the landscape looked like a rock concert just before the band gods emerged on stage. Only the readouts from their handhelds gave them meaningful direction.

Park felt the ground for a soft place and inserted a long stake. A light blinked on the exposed tip, its tempo increasing until it held solid. Park checked his screen.

"The good news is soil and air composition are relatively the same, and, with no ocean impacts and the atmosphere already being so dense, biological life is status quo. Whatever struck us hasn't made Singh any less habitable."

"What's the bad news?"

"That our normal radio interference is going to be compounded until this air clears." Park pulled the composite tester from the soil and tucked it into his suit. "Doesn't change what we need to do though. Let's get to work."

It was a salvage run; they needed parts that could be fashioned together into a transmitter mast. Tethered by a lengthy spool of electrical wire, the men paced in opposite directions. They had no idea which way the wind may have sent their former headquarters. Park turned back after a few steps. Graham was already lost in the particle fog.

"You alright out there, Bloomberg?"

"This would be better with some music."

"You want me to sing?" asked Park.

"Or we could talk." Graham shuffled his feet, scanning the ground for Starseed property. "You're from Caspius, right?"

Park nearly stumbled over a sheet of metal wedged into the rock. It was charred, a corner of it melted away.

"Practically born there," Park said.

"Yet we both ended up in university, both became engineers."

"Right," said Park. "That's my story I guess, a feel good tale about a slum kid overcoming their meager upbringing, blah, blah, blah."

"It's a good story."

"For you, maybe. Stripped down into prose, pressed between two neat covers you can shut and shelve when you're through. It's different for the actual person in the story though. My parents moved to Mars with nothing, less than nothing actually because my father was contracted by the ice haulers before they left home. It's how they could afford the journey. When he stepped onto Mars he was an indentured servant, promised twenty years of his life just so his family could have a *chance* at prosperity."

"Brave," said Graham, squinting at a curved silhouette up ahead.

"Or hopelessly optimistic," Park said.

"It got you into university."

The shape was closer now, the curved outline more defined. The wall was man made.

"*That* twenty. My father agreed to another twenty to pay for my education. He gave up his entire life for me, and what have I done? I have no children. His legacy ends with me."

"Pigshit. Every colony you helped start, all these people will exist and thrive because of your work. That's a pretty solid legacy."

Park stared off into the dust. "Maybe."

"And now you're going to save another colony," said Graham. He ran his gloved hand over the exposed skeletal makeup of the large structure. "I found the cap."

"Oh, good."

"Yeah, and some of the equipment is here too. Banged up obviously, but surprisingly intact. This must be the section we let loose."

"We're just after the beams, but that's good. I'm on my way."

By the time Park had backtracked the cable leading to his anchored colleague, Graham had already disassembled several support beams from inside the cap's severed wall. Park joined in and an hour later they had enough components necessary to build the mast, but Park hesitated. He was examining the panels they were leaving behind.

"Should we take more panels?" asked Graham.

"No," said Park. "I was just checking something." He pointed to the large, blackened sheet beneath the pile of aluminum tubes. "Where did you get that one?"

"Found it off to the side." Graham had drilled two holes in the metal sheet and looped knotted wire through. He tugged at the poor man's sled, showcasing his creation. "Pretty ingenious, right?"

"Yeah." Park did not sound impressed.

"Well, I can't pull this thing myself," said Graham, "and we're losing daylight."

"Right. Let's move."

Reconvened above Singh Tower, the men configured aluminum pieces like a puzzle, welding them together when something fit. Park attached the transmitter to what would be the mast's upright end and together they hoisted it into position. Three electric cables were secured as guy lines, another snaking through an access panel into the tower below.

Graham jumped into the hatch and began connecting the cable's end to the radio console they had rescued from the blasts.

"What do we say?" he yelled up to Park.

"We give them the facts as we know them."

Park stared at Graham's panel sled, a rectangular blotch on Singh's violet surface. It was unusually large, not the typical size or curvature of those used on the cap. Park flipped the burnt sheet over with his foot. It hit the ground with a melodic warble, and Park's eyebrows folded in like they had been magnetized. He raised his head to the stars he could not see, then his watch flashed and chimed. He lowered himself underground and closed the hatch.

Both men removed their suits. They glistened with sweat, odors pungent enough to sting their eyes, but neither concerned themselves over it. Graham toggled the radio on and stepped back. The static was immense.

Graham motioned to the device. "Are you gonna call them or are you waiting for something?"

Clearing his forehead with his sleeve, Park addressed the console and pushed the button on the mic.

"Station, this is Singh Tower. Do you read?"

The static was lively, popping and buzzing, the volume falling to a whisper, then rattling the speaker cover. No one responded. He let the noise carry for a minute, then leaned into the mic again.

"This is Singh Tower, Station. We need to report in. Do you read?"

Static.

"Everything is working, right?" asked Graham.

"You saw me test the transmitter."

"The cables?"

"They're fine."

"It's that dust," Graham said. "There's too much interference."

"Maybe."

"Why aren't you trying again?" asked Graham. "They won't know we need to talk if you don't talk." Graham nudged Park aside and took the mic. "Starseed Station, come in. Please come in."

He let the button loose and closed his eyes, waiting for a voice in the chaos of sound. The station had gone quiet.

"Graham." Park took him by the shoulder. "Look at me. There's something I need to say."

Graham lowered the volume, but only a little. "What?"

"I saw something up top, a panel that had been burned even though we saw no other evidence of fire on the cap floor or on that big chunk of cap wall we found."

"We were down here. An explosion could have happened anywhere during the impacts."

"Perhaps, and I didn't think too much of it at first, but then I saw that big panel we pulled the support pieces on. It had the same burns."

"So what?"

"Well, it's not just the burns. There's something else." Graham shone a light on the nearby tower wall. "Look at these panels. What do they all have in common?"

"They're all the same size, same composite."

"Yes, but what else?"

"Park. I've no interest in this Sherlock Holmes shit. Just tell me what you know!"

"Okay." Park moved closer to the wall, pointing to several spots on each molded metal piece. Everywhere he pointed, the words 'Starseed Property' were embossed into the aluminum. "Every panel in here and on the cap. Every one of them is marked like this, except for those two burned pieces out there."

"And?"

"They didn't come from this facility, Graham. I think they're from Starseed Station. I think something devastating happened up there, and it came down on us. I think the station is what crashed into this planet."

"That's ridiculous. You're ridiculous." Radio static surged. Graham shouted over it. "They could have had to change altitude and we're out of their swath! Hell, the operator could be taking a huge shit for all we know! The station is fine! We keep the radio going and when the dust settles, they'll contact us!"

"That's fine," Park said. "We'll keep it on, I agree, and I hope to hell everything is fine up there, but I saw what I saw and I know what I know, and I know for a fact those pieces didn't come from here."

"How? We make this place operational, but we didn't build the damned thing. You didn't weld all these panels into place."

"No, but I know Starseed, and so do you. Coin and credit, remember?"

"Stamping your name on parts is vanity, not frugality."

"Their frugality is *why* they mark their property. On Mars, my father hauled ice. You know what my mother did? She was a beetle catcher and a trash lark. She scrounged through mounds of filth looking for anything of value we could resell, and Starseed was the major contributor to those trash piles."

"I don't get it."

"You will if you listen. When the population began to swell, not all housing was affordable. Underground shanty towns formed, and guess who had mounds of excess material that was just perfect for keeping out radiation."

"Starseed."

"But then the building associations got peeved they were losing out on new buyers and, since the law there was laughably lacking, those mafia bastards raided shanty towns day after day, terrifying everyone."

"Caspius."

"That's right. You and Sam were safe at New Athens. You don't know a thing about it. May as well have been on opposite sides of the planet."

"But I'd been through Caspius to the east observation center. It was crowded with police."

"It's true. The law finally came to our defense and successfully ran out the mafia, but that was before Starseed began marking every piece of metal that came out of their manufacturing facilities. That was before they declared 'retired' equipment as officially dangerous material. The law sent to help was now hauling us to prison for theft and safety violations."

"That's terrible. I'm sorry."

"Don't worry about it. It's old news."

Graham picked crusted blood from his scalp. "Maybe you know these things, Park, but you don't know what happened to the station. You can't."

"You're right. I'm sorry."

Graham let the static rise and fall, twisting the knob through rarely-used frequencies. "But you think it's gone, don't you?"

Park knelt by his colleague, folding his good arm over the man's shoulder.

"No, Graham. I believe something *happened*, but it's highly unlikely the whole station would be compromised. It's a massive structure divided into multitudes of sections and compartments, each with their own automated lockdown systems. Whatever went wrong was probably contained and mitigated. My guess is their own comms suffered and they're fixing them now. We just have to…"

"Wait?"

"No. Go back."

"To what?"

"Move over," Park said.

Graham cleared himself and Park worked the dials. He twisted the volume knob and slowly turned back through the frequencies. The static chewed the airwaves, gobbling up existence, and then there was something else. It was a beep. A signal. Graham leaned over and cranked the volume to its upper limit.

Static roared as they waited for the tone to repeat. Graham's skin tingled and his ears began to hurt, but he wouldn't back from the speaker.

They waited for what felt like a lifetime. They waited until they both doubted there was anything there to begin with.

Beep.

The engineers looked at one another and smiled.

"Someone's out there!" shouted Graham.

Park nodded. "Someone's alive."

THE SIGNAL WAS A BEACON, but whoever had activated it wasn't answering the radio.

"There are two possibilities," said Park. "The beacon is coming from the station in space or from one of its lifeboats on-planet."

"Lifeboats?" asked Graham. "They wouldn't have used lifeboats unless—"

"Don't worry until there's something to worry about."

The men needed more data, which required more equipment. Park made a list and they put it into action. The men returned to the surface to find the seismograph from the section of dismantled cap. Between the 'Lounge' scrap pile and borrowed tower components, along with some aggressive duct taping, the pair were able to craft what was needed.

"If the life support systems are still running, which they should be, the seismograph sensors will pick up the hum of the machinery on the lifeboat."

"*If* it's a lifeboat," said Graham.

"Right."

The beacon continued its molasses rhythm while Park made adjustments to the seismograph. Moments later he pointed to a jittery line on its cracked screen.

"It's here?"

"Well, it's on Singh, but…" Park mumbled to himself. "Shit. It's far."

"How far?"

Park slumped to the floor. "It would take a full day to walk it. The rover can't get over that terrain and we'd need something big just to haul the oxygen necessary for us to get there and back."

Graham watched the line on the screen, its steady, sawtooth signal bouncing up and down.

"It doesn't matter," said Graham. "If there's a lifeboat here then you were right before. The station is in real trouble."

"We don't know that."

"We don't?" shouted Graham. "If the station was fine, there wouldn't be a fucking lifeboat down here!"

"What I mean, Graham, is we can no longer assume Starseed Station is functional. Frankly, there may be nothing left."

"Highly unlikely! That's what you said, am I wrong?"

Park shook his head. "The use of lifeboats alters my earlier assessment."

Graham's face continued to redden. "You said it was highly unlikely the whole thing could be compromised. Maybe there was a malfunction," said Graham. "Maybe the lifeboat launched itself or somebody panicked too soon and rushed to get off."

"Or the person in that lifeboat is the only survivor. We just don't know." Park sighed. "Let's make a list."

"Fuck your list! We take the shuttle to Station and we find out what really happened!"

"It's an emergency shuttle, Graham."

"Exactly!"

"What I mean is it's designed for a specific purpose, to get us *to* the station. We need to refuel once we get there in order to return to Singh. If we take the shuttle out there and see nothing but empty space, we can't get back. We'll be stranded in space until we die."

"And if the station is only partially damaged? If the life support or the generators or the water filtration need repair and we could help, we'd be leaving over two hundred people in the same dire situation."

"They have their own engineers," said Park. "Highly qualified and competent engineers."

Graham's eyes watered. "It's my family up there, Park. I need to know if they're okay. I need to know what happened."

"You know who could tell us? Whoever is in that lifeboat."

"The person we can't feasibly reach?"

"If we use the shuttle, we could."

"Dammit." Graham wiped his eyes. "You said we can't get there and back."

"We can't get to the *station* and back. We burn too much fuel getting the two of us through the atmosphere. Planetary travel is a whole different beast. We can go out there and bring that person back to the tower with fuel to spare, but…"

"But we won't have enough to reach the station if we need to."

"That's right. It's one or the other."

"Okay." Graham sighed. "Make your list."

Park marked each scenario with a dirty, weathered finger. Few of them left the station in good condition. Fewer still granted the lifeboat survivor a favorable outcome without rescue. Almost all of the outcomes required use of the shuttle. All except one.

"Or we just stay here," said Park. "The station gets repaired and sends someone down for us and for whoever is in that lifeboat."

"And if no one comes?"

"Eventually someone will. Starseed will note the next supply ship returns home as full as when it left and they'll know something is wrong. Meanwhile, we survive down here while we wait, just as the colonists would have, and with only the two of us we'd survive for much longer."

The lonely call of the beacon sounded over the radio.

"We can't just stay here," said Graham.

"So," said Park. "Which is it?"

"Whoever's in that lifeboat needs our help," Graham said, "and maybe they can tell me what happened to my wife and daughter."

"Okay, but it's too dark to leave now. We have to wait until morning. Are you going to be alright with that?"

"What choice do I have?"

That night Graham camped by the radio console. He silenced the beacon, returning to the orbiting station's standard frequency.

At times, voices came through the static, but none were from new broadcasts. There was nothing but Singh's classic time-bending top 40. The historic signals bounced in and out like tourists, Graham's excitement waning more with each revisited transmission. Past Park and Past Operations Director delivered their back and forth, condition confirmations and acknowledgments. 'All is well,' they'd say.

Graham knew Park was asleep in his bed, yet he considered the voices on the radio to be echoes of the dead. They were all just ghosts, lost in the void.

Mina's voice was there too.

"Hey, Dad."

Graham embraced the console, ear pressed to the speaker as he cried. "Hey, kid."

"Is it about you and Mom?" Mina's voice fought through the static. "You're ridiculous. I like botany."

"Yeah," said Graham, "but me and Mister Chen are snap. We can fix what's wrong up there. We can help." Graham let the tears drop onto the machine. "Just tell us if you need help, honey."

The static screamed in his ears, mocking him. The old transmission had moved on. She was gone all over again. Graham put his mouth to the mic and pressed the button.

"Samantha," he whispered. "I'm sorry I'm not there. I'm sorry I didn't listen to you. When this is over, we'll go wherever you want. I'll walk out on my contract with Starseed if I need to. Fuck them. You were right. We should be settling somewhere, spending time as a family before Mina goes off on her own. I want that, and I want to be with you."

He took in a shuddered breath, his vision blurred by tears. "Mina. We didn't really talk about having kids, your Mom and I...."

Graham finished the message to his daughter and returned to the settings where the beacon was strongest. He listened for a few beeps from the man in the lifeboat, then switched off the console.

"You better know something, whoever you are."

THE SHUTTLE WAS in good working order, but the opening above the launch corridor had to be cleared of debris. They parted the loading doors which angled down to the vehicle bay and started the rover without trouble, but even with modifications, the small vehicle was ill-suited as a bulldozer. Hours of daylight were lost, yet the climate of Singh 12-b was heating up.

"All the dust has trapped the heat," said Park. "Get ready to sweat."

"I hope there was plenty of water on that lifeboat," said Graham.

Neither man was a qualified pilot, but they could follow a checklist with astute precision. With data from the seismograph, they determined coordinates for the lifeboat, plugged the numbers in per instruction, and let the ship take them away.

"It's been a while," Park said.

They relied on instruments to guide them through the initial haze, Singh revealing itself in flashes until their dramatic emergence from the dust.

"I've seen more of this planet in the last two days than I have in the year we've been in that tower."

"We'll switch to expedition team for the next colony."

"Hell no," said Graham. "Half those guys don't come back."

They looked to one another with somber faces. There was no need to share what they were thinking.

The shuttle rumbled under their boots. Graham braced himself with Park's chair, both men staring out on the strange world. The faint glow of Singh's sun through the clouds back lit mountains in the distance. A forest of stone-like pillars dotted the ground below. Hues of orange and purple painted the jagged, undulating landscape. It was inarguably beautiful.

"There's something I don't understand," said Graham.

"Why work for Starseed if they treated your people so poorly?"

Park sighed. "Honest man's revenge I guess. Forced redemption. Quite a few of us went that route, securing jobs with the enemy. We used their money to improve our little town, and eventually Caspius became a self-made community, mafia and Starseed be damned. Quiet victories, I guess."

"I guess."

"Anyway. It got me off Mars."

Graham's handheld alerted him they had neared the source of the beacon. He nudged Park, but the shuttle's thrusters were already adjusting. The entire craft twisted into an upright position and began falling back to the surface. The men's stomachs turned and the controlled bursts of the landing system jolted them until they struck ground.

Restraints undone and exit checklist completed, the two stepped down onto new territory. The heat was instant and the suits felt even heavier than normal. The landing zone was solid, yet sprouts like dried coral emerged from cracks in the surface.

"Look," said Park.

Graham followed the man's finger to something just visible around a rocky outcrop. The lifeboat was curved like a giant almond, its lower tip wedged into Singh's crust. The top third was lit up like a lighthouse. Its metal sides were scorched. The door was missing. The outcome was already evident. No one was inside.

Graham circled the craft. There were no tracks, no blood, nothing to indicate a person had ever been present.

"But the beacon," said Graham.

Park stepped in the tight space of the lifeboat, surveying miniature consoles. "I was afraid of this." He flicked a switch and the intermittent tone ceased. The light atop the sloped roof went dark. "I think the beacon activation was just part of the landing sequence."

"Or the person left when no one came," said Graham. "Would they have a radio on them?"

"Maybe something short range like our helmet comms."

Graham headed back to the shuttle and activated its radio. It was static like the one at the tower.

"Is anyone out there? Come back. Hello!"

"Stop!" yelled Park. "Look here." He had opened an interior panel. "There's no coolant, no oxygen, and the whole damned door is missing. No one could have lived if they escaped in this heap."

Park struck one of the consoles, cracking its face. "Son of a bitch!" He kicked the tiny bench where a passenger was supposed to sit. He freed his hammer from his tool belt and smashed the controls. "Cheap, Starseed fucks! You killed us all, didn't you?" He kicked and he hammered and he cursed. "We gave everything to you and you couldn't even keep the lifeboats intact?"

His hammer pierced the shell of the craft and something burst. Park was thrown. Graham ran to him, nearly tumbling over top the felled engineer.

"Park! What happened?"

"What?"

Park's eyes were wide. He coughed, and blood splattered the inside of his helmet.

"Oh, shit," said Graham.

He rolled the man onto his side and Park screamed.

"Stop!" He groaned. "My ribs. I think they're broken."

A hole was in Park's oxygen tank. "Something hit your tank."

"I saw bolts flying."

Park spat up more blood.

"They must have been holding back pressure from something. More cheap parts I bet. We'll get you back to the tower. Come on."

"No, no, no." Park shoved himself onto his back and reached for his helmet.

"Stop that!" shouted Graham.

The broken engineer swatted his colleague. "I can't breathe!"

He freed the helmet clasps, but couldn't twist it loose with one hand. "Please," said Park. "Help me."

"The oxygen is too low here." Graham removed Park's helmet, tossing it aside. "Let me get you in the shuttle."

Park smiled. "Yeah. I'm sorry, Graham, but I'm not going anywhere."

"Park. You'll die."

He nodded. "I know."

Park coughed and grunted, angered by the pain. Graham wiped blood from his friend's face.

"I'm so sorry," said Graham. "We came out here for nothing."

"We tried." He grabbed hold of Graham's shoulders. His gaze was distant, almost absent. "Baba," Park said. "I'm sorry. I tried to honor you, sir. I really did."

Graham pulled him near.

"Don't leave me out here," whispered Graham, but Park was already dead.

GRAHAM HELD his companion until dusk crept in. There were no crickets to mark the evening, no critters scampering back to their dens. With no leaves to rustle or bushes to shake, even the wind was peacefully muted. All was quiet apart from the shuttle's radio static. Graham looked up at the sky, hoping even a single star would penetrate Singh's atmospheric ceiling. There was nothing. Park was gone, and so was everyone on the station.

Then the static ceased.

"Dad!"

The repeat broadcast taunted him, even out here. He didn't want the memory. Not now.

"Dad! Where are you?"

"What?"

He let Park slip from his grasp. This was not some past message resurfacing. It was his daughter. She was alive. Graham stumbled to the shuttle, smashing the mic button so hard something sparked beneath. He shouted through giddy tears.

"Mina! I'm here! Where are you?"

The static returned.

"No! Don't you do this to me!" He pressed the button again. "Zarmina! It's Dad! Are you alright?"

More static.

He fell into the seat, flipping switches and turning dials, Park's blood smearing over the console. He squeezed his fists, wringing red from his gloved fingertips.

"It was real," he whispered. "She was there, I know it." Graham activated the mic again. "Mina! It's Dad. I'm here! Is the station repaired? Are you and Mom okay?"

The static paused in response, but the voice that came through was incredibly faint.

"…help," she said.

Graham sat up. "They're still up there, Park. How do I get to them?"

Park spoke in his mind: "Make a list."

Graham looked at the controls. The fuel was half empty; there wasn't enough to breach the atmosphere.

"One," he said. "Fuel."

He looked in the space behind him. They had filled it with extra oxygen in case the survivor had none.

"I can use the oxygen to boost the thrusters, but it might not be enough." He looked at Park laying on the rocks. "Of course. The fuel you estimated was based on *two* men. I can get up," he said, "but I have no coordinates. Two. Coordinates."

Something lit up the dark outside, a flash and double chime. It was Park's watch, the alarm for Station's scheduled broadcast range.

"Yes! They'll be coming over the tower soon."

Graham pulled his gloves off and stabbed buttons on the navigation console, reversing their path from Singh Tower. Altering the altitude, he configured the shuttle to get him through the atmosphere to intercept the incoming station. With any luck they'd spot him and guide him into one of the docks.

"I'm coming, Mina."

With coordinates fixed, Graham wielded his torch. In just a few minutes he had fitted the oxygen tanks to the line fueling the thrusters.

Graham sealed the door, cinched his belt, and initiated the launch sequence from memory. The shuttle shook so violently on takeoff he thought he'd left a piece of it behind.

The angle was steep and he moved fast. Heftier particles still lingering from the shockwave blasts threatened to puncture the cockpit, but it wouldn't matter. It was this shuttle's final flight.

The fuel gauge dropped. Alarms desperately called out for attention. Lights were flashing. Graham shut his eyes and ignored it all. He flew into the storm this time, blind and defiant. An unknown object collided with his ship, sending him into a spin. He screamed and cursed, the ship firing stabilizers from multiple angles. When the dizzy spell passed and the roar of the shuttle quieted, Graham opened his eyes.

Stars twinkled in the black. He had made it off Singh 12-b, but Starseed Station wasn't there.

He silenced the alarms and slapped a sparking wire. The radio static was gone and so was Mina's voice. He turned the knobs. Nothing came through. Console readouts were blank. Fuel was at zero. Graham removed his helmet and pinched the bridge of his nose.

"Did I miss it?"

He could hear something on the ship leaking into space. He knew without inspecting the readouts that it was his oxygen.

His vision began to blur, but he spotted something moving in the dark. He leaned ahead to catch a glimpse of the object when a massive structure floated into view. It turned and glistened, its color and curve so familiar, yet so foreign. It was the station, and it was irrevocably destroyed.

Severed shafts and absent walls exposed interior rooms and compartments of the station like museum dioramas, each scene a still of devastation. Fire had clearly ravaged the entire facility. Corpses that weren't burned into the walls were floating in space, skin like iced-over charcoal.

He watched it drift, continuing on its orbit like it had for a year, like it might for the rest of time. With each new section that passed he hoped for some indication that a pocket of life remained, but he knew the system. He knew the machinery and what was needed to sustain human life. All of it was broken.

Graham sobbed, and in his grief he heard his daughter's voice again.

"Dad. I don't know if you can hear me…."

Graham smeared his eyes and blinked in spasms, searching for Mina.

"Mina!" Graham shouted into the burnt-out mic.

Darkness pressed on him, creeping past his eyes and into his mind. He struggled against its invasive lull, but his body had already abandoned him. He sank into his chair and shut his eyes.

Mina.

"I don't know if you can hear me," she said, "but I'm safe. I made it off the station."

"Mina," he whispered, uncertain if he had spoken the words aloud. "You're alive."

The stars were too bright now. He was adrift amongst their light.

———

MINA SAT on the walkway beneath the hatch, twisting the dials on the radio console.

"Dad. I don't know where you are but I'm here in Singh Tower. I made it. You'd have been proud of me, Dad. I took the tanks from the lifeboat, dragged them behind me using the door. It was a long walk, but I made it."

She let the mic button loose to static, then tried again.

"Me and a few others got to the lifeboats but I lost track of them after. I lost track of Mom. I'm sorry." She rubbed her sleeve across her face. "I'll wait here for you both," she said.

Mina sat by the radio, searching the din for voices. Finally, her father answered.

"We didn't really talk about having kids," Graham said.

Mina gripped the mic and shouted. "Dad! Where are you?"

Graham's broadcast continued. "We were young adventurers, you know? Science geek adventurers, but adventurers none-the-less. All we wanted was to go deep into space, where people hadn't been before."

"Daddy?"

Her father's voice came in and out through the atmospheric buzz, never responding to her, never answering her pleas. Mina understood this wasn't her Dad, at least not the Graham Bloomberg of the present. She understood somehow that he was gone, that this was the last of him, and she wept.

"When Sam got pregnant," Graham said, "a lot changed. *We* changed, and it wasn't always easy, but no matter what complexities came our way, we were just so damned excited to have you with us. I've enjoyed being your father, Mina. Spending time with you. Seeing you become an intelligent, headstrong young woman. You're wonderful, better than I thought any kid of mine would ever be."

The rhythmic hums and clicks of machinery filled the hollow tunnels of Singh Tower, her father's well-oiled machine. Mina increased the radio volume and descended to the biotech labs. She needed to see her mother's plants.

Graham's voice echoed throughout the tower. "All these colonies we've helped establish, all the families we've helped start their own beginnings, that's what it's all been about. It was never about us. It's always been about the future of people. Of humanity. Of you. *You* were our true adventure."

Mina stared at the nascent life sprouting through mounds of foreign soil, crying in the violescent glow of the hybrid leaves so eager to unfurl.

Static mixed with Graham's shaking breaths. "We've told you the origin of your name."

Mina rolled her eyes.

"Don't roll your eyes, because I'm going to tell you again."

She chuckled and cleared her tears.

"Zarmina was a planet whose very existence was argued over by scientists for decades," said Graham. "When deep-space travel was finally invented, scientists went out there and discovered the truth for themselves. They proved something was real when so many said it wasn't. Nobody really *knows* what's out there, and sometimes I think it's better that way. The adventure is in the journey *to* the discovery, and wherever you are now…"

She heard her father cry, struggling to regain composure.

"Wherever you're going," his voice was shaking, "relish in the adventure of it, okay?"

"Okay, Daddy."

"I love you, daughter," her father said. "I love you always."

"I love you too," she said.

Graham vanished only to be replaced by Mister Chen and someone from the station, more voices in the void. The disembodied men chatted over figures and status conditions. Mister Chen made lists.

Mina picked up a handheld and navigated through graphs and binary readouts, trying to follow along. In these past broadcasts Singh Tower was a model of efficiency and mechanical splendor, but things had changed.

The planet had been barraged with Starseed debris. The cap was gone. Despite the efforts of its former engineers, the tower needed repairs.

She pressed a finger to the signature square and opted to edit her profile. The line for 'Home' had always been blank. Mina had lived on two colonies and a space station and considered taking extended shelter in a cave when struggling to find the tower, but she had found it.

She had found it, and with some luck and a beacon from the makeshift radio tower, other survivors would find it too. She typed 'Singh 12-b,' then scrolled to the line marked 'Occupation.' She deleted 'Student' and entered 'Bio-technician / Engineer,' and saved the changes.

Checklist indicators on her handheld were flashing, and flashing lights meant bad news. That's what her father had told her. Zarmina clicked on the first item.

There was work to be done before the others arrived.

About Matt Sully

Matt C. Sully studied journalism at Texas A&M, igniting his love for wordcraft. He has explored storytelling methods from screenplays to novels and regularly features short stories on his blog, MattCSully.com, along with general writing tips and updates.

His love for film is expressed through the film review and pitch podcast, *Movie Retakes* (available on all major podcast platforms and MovieRetakes.com).

His personal journey has taken him from the southern United States to now residing in Ontario, Canada with his wonderful, inspirational wife and daughter.

He is currently seeking publication for his first novel, Father's Creed, a historical fiction adventure about the clash of native and Anglo cultures set against the backdrop of the War of 1812.

The Thing with Feathers

Lara Bujold Clouden

Another new school. Another town. An unstable mother. It's enough to make anyone a little crazy, so when supernatural beings begin to appear, Jen is left wondering: Are things getting better, or much, much worse?

The Thing with Feathers

Lara Bujold Clouden

The dog wasn't in his usual place under Jen's bed. Worried Toby might have gotten out and become lost in the new neighborhood, Jen slipped on her sandals and crept down the carpeted stairs, taking care not to wake her parents or her younger brother.

She found Toby soon enough, thumping his tail on the kitchen floor in front of the door. He lumbered to his feet and waited pointedly, his old-man eyebrows beseeching her to let him out. With a sigh, she took the leash off the hook and snapped it on Toby's collar. The woods behind the house were unlit and uninviting this time of night, but she didn't trust Toby to find his way alone. Holding the screen door to keep it from banging shut, Jen walked across the yard. The moist grass wiped across her bare heels as she made her way to the path at the edge of the woods.

A light broadcasting into the sky over an area deeper in the woods made the path less formidable.

Toby perked up his ears and fluffy tail, sniffing the night air and investigating tree roots and foliage. As the dog squatted in the brush, a faint chord of electronic music caught Jen's attention. When Toby finished, Jen followed the sound.

The music grew clearer as she drew nearer to its source, but she did not recognize the tune. Maybe it was a rave? She looked down, chewing the inside of her cheek. Her Superwoman t-shirt had been big on her five years ago but was now unflatteringly snug across her arms and belly. If her new classmates were out here, this outfit had the potential to be excruciatingly embarrassing. Maybe she could see what was happening without being noticed.

A cloying herbal scent drifted in the air. Marijuana? No, it was closer to gingerbread. She made her way toward the boom of the bass, and after a bend in the path, found the going easier. A field light left stark shadows across the path.

Just as she arrived at a clearing, Toby barked.

The sound stopped.

Lights extinguished.

A fluttering of many wings, loud as a helicopter, surrounded her. Jen covered her ears with her forearms, using her hands to protect her head from the unknown source of chaos. It lasted a few moments, then, silence.

Something croaked, possibly a voice, but too far away for Jen to understand.

She stood a few seconds longer, unable to shake the sense that multiple beings watched her—waiting and listening in the dark.

"Hey," she called in a small voice, then cleared her throat. "Anybody out there?"

She wavered between hope and the fear that someone would respond.

Toby whimpered.

"Shhh!" Jen scolded, whispering, "I don't think they like dogs."

Her forearms and the back of her neck tingled where tiny hairs rose. With a shudder, she felt her way toward the path back home. A branch scraped her cheek and she stopped, cursing when her fingertips detected a silky smear of blood from the burning cut.

Jen heard the croaking sound again, louder this time and definitely a voice, but still unintelligible. Another invisible voice sounded. Jen stood, frozen in place, unsure now whether the voices were in front or behind her on the dark, uneven path. A puff of warmth, downy soft and feathery, touched the scratch on Jen's face. She flinched away from it, ducking and putting up her hands to ward off an expected onslaught.

Although no attack came, a wave of adrenaline rocked her. She looked around, eyes wide, trying to see. Her feet seemed rooted to the ground. It occurred to her it would be hard to run in these sandals. Again, the feathery thing bumped her cheek like a moth against a lamp. Fear rose in her, clouding her vision. Gradually, it began to subside, and only then did she notice the sting on her cheek had dissipated.

Toby growled. The warm thing retreated with a flutter, leaving behind a waft of the spicy scent she had noticed earlier.

She investigated her face and, finding it dry and painless, called out in a quavering voice, "Uh, thanks?"

At least these weren't vampires, she thought. Then she realized there had been blood on her face, and *now it was gone.* Oh God, was that a bat? The knowledge sent a jolt coursing through her, and the beings rustled, so quickly it seemed almost in response to her emotions. They nestled close to her, bussing her cheeks and bare arms with their soft, fuzzy bodies until her heartbeat returned to a normal pace. Bats didn't have feathers, and these things seemed to be entirely round in shape. Feathered, but she could detect no wings. Toby growled again and the things fluttered away, emitting another cloud of scent.

Clove! she realized with relief. It smelled like the balls she and her brother made by poking cloves into oranges at Christmas. Her mother kept one hanging in the closet.

Toby strained the leash and Jen allowed him to pull, stumbling behind him, until she finally paused to let him off the leash. He ran back toward the light of the kitchen and away from the disorienting darkness of the woods. The back door slammed in the distance, and she relaxed, knowing someone had let him in. She followed, picking her way more carefully. The closer she came to her grassy yard, the less she believed what had just happened.

"Sally. Stop it! Give me that!"

Toby yelped. Jen picked up the pace, racing through the backyard. She tore open the back door.

The sounds of a struggle came from the living room.

Something fell. The hall table? Another yelp from Toby and heavy breathing as the struggle continued. Jen peered around the corner into the gloom.

Her father held her mother from behind, his arms reaching around her, one grasping her tight, the other trying to take hold of her arm. Light caught on something shiny. Jen could see a knife in her mother's hand.

Her mother's other hand held Toby by the scruff of the neck, and Toby was scrabbling to get away from her.

Jen gasped. Her dad looked up, then said gruffly, "Go, go!" and jutted his chin towards the stairs in dismissal. His hands were still tightly bound around Jen's mother.

Jen ran up the stairs, averting her eyes instinctively, as if somehow not seeing *them* would hide *her*. She turned around at the top of the staircase, clutched the handrail and leaned over to watch them.

Her parents continued to struggle until her dad finally wrenched her mother's body away from the dog. Toby bounded up the stairs, shot past Jen, and flew under her bed, reduced to a small, quivering nose under the dust ruffle.

Jen ran to Timmy's bedroom. He was sound asleep, his arm draped across the top of his head. She locked his door from the inside and went through their shared bathroom to get to her own room. She locked her door too, went to the bed, and lifted the dust ruffle to peer at Toby. The dog backed away from her, shivering.

"It's okay, boy," she said in what she hoped was a soothing voice. "I've got you. Come here, that's a good boy."

But try as she would, the dog would not budge. Jen crawled into bed. Her parents' voices rose and fell, each pleading with the other.

"No, Mark! I can't stand them! They make me feel like a zombie," her mother wailed.

"You can't just stop taking the pills. They keep you safe. They keep *us* safe!"

"I know it seems bad—"

"Bad?" he echoed, cutting her off. "Come on, Sally. You have to see how unhinged you are. Jesus, the dog…" Jen's dad's voice trailed off. Was he crying or was exasperation finally getting to him? Jen winced and her stomach roiled.

She pulled her cheap, flat pillow over her ear, mashing it to muffle the sound. The pillow was terrible for everything else but was great for noise canceling. It was hot and her pulse pounded in her ear until it felt like an internal organ. It was a long time before she fell back asleep.

It was even longer before she began making sense of that night.

―――

A YEAR LATER, Jen stood surveying her closet. Yet another new start, she thought. She was glad she had unpacked and set up her room when they arrived last week; the rest of the house was littered with moving boxes. She still burned with rage when she thought about Toby, and the lame excuses her father had made about keeping him back in Virginia until they "settled in." Her idiotic brother still believed the dog would join them. Jen knew it had nothing to do with transportation and everything to do with her bugged out mother.

She dressed for school, carefully selecting an outfit that would keep her cool in the late summer heatwave, yet manage to cover her pale, meaty upper arms. No doubt the girls here were just as waifish as the ones back in Virginia, where Jen was used to being ignored, if not shunned. She picked a soft T-shirt that covered her tummy roll without clinging to it, and a pair of khaki cargo shorts. Grabbing her camouflage backpack, Jen made her way down to the kitchen. She found her brother at the breakfast table, his face hidden behind a box of cereal.

"Is there any left?" she asked.

"Good morning, Jen, how did you sleep?" Her mother was standing at the sink, holding a cup of coffee.

"Fine." Jen kept her eyes on the kitchen table. "Can I have some cereal?"

"There should be enough," Jen's mother said. "Timmy? Could you make room for your sister, please?"

Timmy picked up the box. "I'm reading the puzzle on the back."

Jen's mother started to chastise him, but Jen spoke over her. "Can't you just let me hold it for a second?"

"No, I'm doing the puzzle."

"You could care less about puzzles. Just give me the cereal."

"I'm busy with this one." His reedy voice, firm with indignation, grated on Jen's ears and she growled at him.

Jen's mother crossed the kitchen, plucked the box out of his hand, and carried it to the cupboard, firmly shutting the door with a frown.

"Stop bickering, both of you."

"Mooooom," they began in harmony, but she was having none of it.

"Have the eggs I made, and no whining either."

Jen wanted to point out this injustice, but thought better of it, instead sitting down roughly on the bench next to her brother, shoving him with her hip. His head turned quickly, mouth open, eyes narrowed in what Jen recognized as his wounded martyr face. After a glance at his mother, he remained silent.

Jen took a piece of toast and dished herself some scrambled eggs.

"What do you two have on today?" her mother asked in a sweet voice, as if neither of them were slouching in sullen protest.

"First day of school!" Timmy exclaimed, aghast.

Timmy's apparent shock irritated Jen. He still couldn't tell when their mother was out of it.

"Is Dad driving us?" she asked.

Her mother sipped her coffee.

"Mom?"

"Good morning, Jen, how did you sleep?" her mother said.

"Fine. Is Dad up yet?"

Timmy started humming to himself.

"Mom?" Jen asked gently. "Is Dad driving us to school today?"

"Who's calling my name?" Jen's dad filled the doorway, a mock scowl on his bearded face.

Relief filled Jen and she beamed at her father. "*I'm* calling you. Can you drive us to school?"

"Don't you want to ride your bikes?"

"Dad." Both children glared at him.

"Maybe tomorrow then. Fine, I'll drive you. Where's the cereal?"

Jen and Timmy looked expectantly at their mother, but she was all innocence.

"Better stick to eggs and toast." Jen gave her dad a

meaningful glance and tipped her head towards her mother, who continued to sip her coffee with a vacant expression.

"I see," he said quietly. "Right then. Jen, dish me up the rest of those eggs. Sally, would you pour me a cup of coffee? Do we have any cream?"

"Mark, you're not supposed to take cream," Jen's mother said, her back to them as, without hesitation, she opened the fridge to take out the cream.

"That is correct." Jen's dad dragged the kitchen chair from the table and loaded his wide girth onto the worn wooden seat. "What else can't I have?" His eyes twinkled at Jen. "Got any donuts?"

Jen snorted and passed him his plate of eggs. "Here. Have some cholesterol."

"I want some collecteral!" Timmy's outrage softened as he studied the plate. "What's collecteral? That looks like eggs."

Jen and her dad exchanged a wry smile, but neither explained to Timmy. It was best to nip "question time" in the bud and ignore him.

"Dad, hurry up and eat that, I want to get there early and scout out the lay of the land."

"Why? Are you going to war?"

"Yes. It's called high school."

"Oh. Well in that case, let me get these down so we can do battle."

The room quieted to the sound of fork on plate as Jen's dad tucked into the eggs. He seemed unperturbed by the audience, and finished quickly, washing it down with a long sip of steaming coffee.

"Doesn't that burn your mouth?" Timmy asked.

"Yep." Jen's dad set the mug down firmly and lifted himself out of the chair with a grunt. "Into the car, little learners. The bus is leaving."

"'Bye." Jen's mom waved at them, without leaving her place at the sink.

The Thing with Feathers

"I'll be back in a few, Sally," Jen's dad said, pausing in the doorway.

Jen's mom smoothed a lock of gray hair behind one ear, then clasped her arms around herself tightly. "You don't need to do that."

Her dad seemed about to reply, but instead, shut his mouth and hustled Timmy out the door, calling over his shoulder, "See you in a jiffy!"

Jen hefted her backpack onto one shoulder and followed her dad and brother out to the car. As she opened the front passenger door, a prism of light danced across the driveway. She held the door still, wondering if it was the cause of the reflection, but the little rainbow continued to flicker its way down the drive. She looked up at the neighbor's window. The curtain was closed.

As the prism winked its way onto the grass and disappeared, a clove-scented breeze stirred the leaves on the driveway. Jen lowered herself into the seat and shut the car door. Her dad turned on the news and pulled out of the driveway.

When he dropped her off in front of the school, Jen's dad dipped his head down and raised his bushy eyebrows at her, holding her eyes in reassurance, she supposed. He smirked and told her not to break too many hearts.

"I don't want any pining boys on my doorstep tomorrow morning. Be judicious with that smile."

She grinned and he pointed at her. "That one!" He clutched his chest in mock pain. "Keep it under wraps, babe, that's a killer."

"Thanks, Dad. You are a mighty dork."

He tipped an imaginary hat to her, and she nodded and slammed the car door. As her nerves quelled for the briefest of moments, she braced herself for the view. The school was a wide brick structure facing the morning sun. Students streamed around her up the steps, ignoring her and looking purposeful. She put on her own similar mask and made her way up and through the entrance.

In the hallways no one seemed to notice her, but when she entered her first-period classroom, the students in the room stopped talking and looked up expectantly.

A girl with long, straight blond hair, perfect pink skin and wide blue eyes looked Jen up and down before dismissing her and resuming her conversation with a tall, brown-skinned girl with impeccable makeup. Jen felt sweaty and plain. She looked for a seat, hoping it would swallow her body and disguise her in some way. She chose the one in the back, next to the window.

On the windowsill, near some young adult books, she spotted another prism. This one was dancing in a serpentine path around the books. Jen looked around to see if anyone else noticed, but the students had resumed their quiet conversations. The colorful light made its way towards her, landing on the desk and drawing a sweeping circle before it disappeared.

In its place came the feathery thing. Its soft, warm body landed on her shoulder and nestled under her chin. In panic, she tried to brush it away. She had last felt these downy creatures that night a year ago in the woods, and the strong scent of clove brought a flood of disturbing memories from that strange dreamlike night.

And then the thing spoke.

"Relax," it said in a low, surprisingly masculine voice.

Jen jerked back, trying to see what was touching her neck, but the thing was invisible. Holding her head still in an effort not to be noticed by her classmates, Jen moved her eyes to her right to see if the girl next to her had heard anything. The girl was engaged in banter with a boy.

"Settle," said the feathered thing. "Breathe."

Jen took in a shaky breath. "Go. Away," she muttered.

The girl next to her turned, gave her the once over and raised an eyebrow, before turning back to her conversation.

Great, Jen thought. Nutty new girl, at your service.

The feathery thing purred. "Be you. They will sort themselves out accordingly."

Again she thought back to that night, and her mother's behavior. Jen had been angry for a long time. Her mother was so weird. So flakey, and so embarrassing. And now here Jen was, haunted by alien moth-beings. Making friends was going to be a piece of cake here, she thought to herself sarcastically. A piece of fruitcake, maybe. A chuckle burbled in the back of Jen's throat, drawing another suspicious glance from the flirting girl.

Jen lifted a hand casually to her neck to stroke the soft body. It purred again.

The door opened and a middle-aged woman with curly red hair entered. The soft thing under Jen's fingertips vanished with a barely audible whisper. "Be you."

The teacher took roll call, and when Jen heard her name, she raised her hand with confidence. "Present."

That night the family ate a macaroni and ground beef hot dish in an almost normal evening. Jen was more talkative than usual, although she kept an eye peeled for more rainbows moving around the floor. Her mother was uncharacteristically focused and alert.

"I was thinking, we should have a dinner party," her mother said to her father, whose widened eyes belied his casual response.

"Sounds good, Honey." He directed his attention to Jen. "So, tell us about your first day of school."

"No, I mean it," her mother persisted. "We could invite

the Hendersons from across the street. They seem nice. I could make enchiladas."

"Enchiladas? You buried the lede. I'm all in on this plan." Jen's dad crinkled his eyes at his wife, mimicking his natural smile, but he couldn't hide the sadness in his gaze. Like Jen, he obviously didn't trust the duration of her mother's lucid moments.

"I learned a new song at school today," Timmy said.

"What's it called?" Jen spoke in a derisive tone out of habit.

"I don't remember," Timmy mumbled, looking down at his plate.

"Was it 'Achy, Breaky, Heart'?" Jen's dad prompted. "Or 'Beans, Beans, The Magical Fruit'?"

Timmy laughed, and a piece of macaroni fell out of his mouth onto his plate, making him laugh harder. He was such an easy mark. "No, Dad," he scolded, still giggling. "They don't sing about tooting in school."

"What! Where are my hard-earned tax dollars going, then? I'm calling your teacher. What's her name?"

"Mrs. Fava."

Jen's dad snorted. "You're kidding me."

"No," Timmy said.

"Your teacher, who refuses to teach you the fart song, is named after the biggest bean in nature?" Jen's dad erupted in a full-blown laugh, pounding the table as he was wracked with mirth.

In the face of his helplessness, the others had to join in.

With a sigh, they finally settled back down and got back to eating, finishing the casserole with a series of sighs, and setting each other off from time to time with a random "Toot!" or suggesting other possible bean relatives of Timmy's teacher.

When Jen's mother stood to clear the table, Jen's dad assigned Jen to "KP duty" with her mother. She did not protest, wanting to talk to her mom while she was still doing well. She waited until the boys left the room.

They worked quietly for a while. Wiping the table studiously, Jen finally spoke.

"So you seem, um, happy tonight."

Jen's mom looked directly at her, pausing with a plate in her hand. "I know it's hard, Jen. I wish I could be there for you all the time. It's just, the medication makes me… well, it's hard to focus. And then when I don't take it, a lot of my concentration goes to keeping 'Them' at bay."

Jen was surprised. No one in the family, and certainly not her mother, ever talked openly about what ailed her. "Them? Do you mean voices?"

"Sometimes." Jen's mother resumed her work, scraping the contents of the plate into the garbage can. "Sometimes it's just a feeling, but it doesn't come from me."

"Do they tell you to do bad things, like when you tried to go after Toby?" Jen asked, her voice tight as her heart pulsed in her throat. She swallowed. "Did they ever tell you to hurt me or Timmy?"

"No!" Her mother's response came out sharp, and she tried to soften it with a crooked smile. "No," she said more gently. "Nothing like that. They are more," she paused, searching, "just the wrong kind of messages."

"Doesn't the medicine help?"

Jen's mother slumped a little. "I guess. But I don't like to take it."

Irritation welled up in Jen. "Well, why not?"

"It's just that, sometimes…" She fixed pleading eyes on Jen. "Sometimes, They are helpful. That's how it started, you know. I was just about your age, and really needed someone to take my side. I didn't have a dad like yours." Jen's mom became wistful. "You're so lucky."

Jen ignored her mom's reverie. "But you could be normal all the time." She saw how this hurt her mother but persisted.

"I mean, what if you mistake the good voices for one of the bad ones? What about when they tell you to do something horrible? What about Toby?"

Jen's mom looked defeated, but still a little defiant. "That won't happen again. I know the difference," she said. "Besides, the good ones have a scent."

Jen knew immediately what her mother's next words would be, and she wanted to plug her ears, but she didn't.

"The good ones smell like cloves."

About Lara Bujold Clouden

Lara Bujold Clouden is a writer living in Connecticut with her husband, two children, and two dogs, some of whom are Caribbean. She also cares for a flock of very pretty, not very smart hens, who provide copious amounts of eggs and occasional violent nourishment for the local fox population.

Born in Duluth, MN, Lara has lived in New York, Paris and the San Francisco Bay Area, and worked as a modern dancer, desktop publisher, business analyst, and communications strategist. She has published a book of short, quirky, mystical fairytales and stories called *A Hankering for Lettuce*, which you can find on Scribl.com as an audiobook and ebook.

Lara is currently working on a full-length novel about a depressed dragon and a sociopathic flower maiden— a genre I think we can all agree is sorely lacking in today's literature.

Lara blogs under the name Elby Cloud at elbycloud.Wordpress.com. You can find her on Twitter at @elbycloud.

The Cursed Memory

Peter Smith

Imagine the ability to remember everything: the good, the bad, and the deadly.

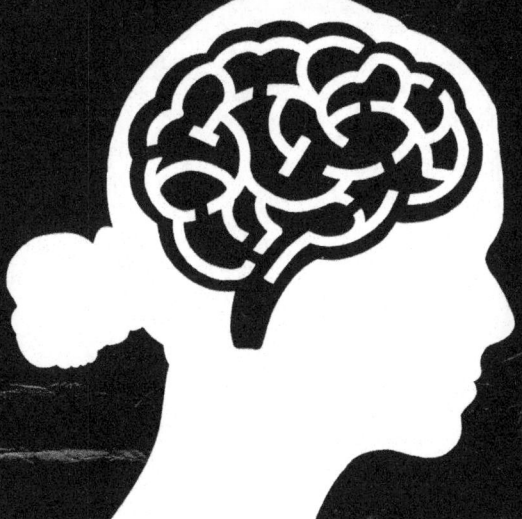

The Cursed Memory

Peter Smith

The sand underfoot was soft and unusually warm for autumn. Wearing a skirt and blazer, Kathy carried her shoes while Becky enjoyed the comfort of jeans, a sweatshirt, and sneakers.

Though Queen Elizabeth was perhaps generous in proclaiming Goderich 'Canada's prettiest town', the view of sunset across Lake Huron explained some of her zeal.

As the sisters plodded along the beach, Kathy asked, "Do you remember much about living here as a kid?"

"Not like you do." Becky winked.

"Seriously."

Becky scanned the scenery. "Not much. One year as a seven-year-old didn't leave much of an impression. How about you? Are at least *some* of your memories positive?"

"Not a lot. It's hard to see past the bullying."

They strolled in silence for a minute, watching the last sliver of sun on the horizon.

"Do you think tomorrow you'll finally be called in?" asked Becky.

Kathy sighed. "I sure hope so. Either way, I was told to be at the courthouse at 8:30 again. I just want to get it over with.

It's ironic, though, that a few months ago I was upset that we hadn't sold Mom's condo yet, but it's turned out to be a Godsend to have somewhere familiar to stay during the trial."

Becky rubbed her sister's back. "We should get going."

THE FOLLOWING MORNING, Judge Hawkins sat hunched over the case file. He tugged at his beard, its grey whiskers meandering north of his sideburns. It was day three of the retrial, but he still couldn't believe it had been ordered based on such flimsy new evidence: a hotshot pathologist disputing the cause of wounds photographed on the accused; and a new witness, claiming to have information regarding a person of interest from 2002.

Fortunately, thanks to mismatched lawyers, the outcome was a foregone conclusion. Hawkins had his money on Crown Attorney Carl Deakin, a legend in criminal prosecution. He was creative, tenacious, and always navigated the courtroom Goldilocks zone: assertive enough to get his point across to the jury, but not aggressive enough to insult their intelligence. His opponent on defense was the rookie, Brenda Cairns, a glorified librarian. Deakin was eating her alive.

After jotting a few final notes on a large yellow pad, Hawkins took a sip of cold coffee and stared through the wall. Despite his confidence in the outcome, he was still stressed. Like half the local population, he remembered the child well, and it made him queasy to envision the lifeless, naked twelve-year-old in the woods outside town. Though no DNA evidence was discovered, the coroner stated that she had clearly been sexually assaulted, and, based purely on circumstantial evidence, a young warehouse worker had paid with his freedom.

Hawkins wasn't involved in the original trial two decades ago because, at the time, he was still trudging down the long

The Cursed Memory

road to *becoming* a judge. However, he had taken time off his corporate law job, and sat in on the proceedings to see how the seasoned Judge Tom Brooks handled the case.

That original trial, though mercifully short, turned out to be one for the ages, with a packed courtroom and heightened police presence to quell vitriol between the families. Even after the trial, acrimony lingered in the community over the rushed judgment, and, according to Judge Brooks's family, that trial was the reason his heart gave out six months later.

The *retrial*, so far, had been comparatively calm, owing largely to the absence of the victim's parents—father deceased; mother institutionalized with dementia. Still, for Hawkins, the end couldn't come soon enough. He took a final swallow of coffee, pulled on his gown, and said a silent prayer.

IN THE HALL outside the courtroom sat thirty-year-old Kathy wearing shoulder-length brown hair, modest business attire and a trace of makeup. Passersby could be forgiven for assuming her name was Jane Q Public, but her unremarkable exterior belied an astounding talent.

While fidgeting with a button on her sleeve, Kathy's stomach gurgled in protest of the morning's meager breakfast of dry toast and ginger tea. Despite already experiencing appeals court months ago, she knew that *this* courtroom would have a jury and a larger crowd of observers. She smoothed her skirt and said, "This outfit makes me look like a pear."

Without looking up from her paperback novel, Becky said, "You look fine."

Kathy closed her eyes and thought back to the sequence of events that led to her involvement in the case. It began when her widowed mother, Gwen, wanting to be closer, but not too close, to her daughters in Toronto, had moved from

Nova Scotia to Goderich, where they'd spent a year of Kathy's childhood.

Tragically, soon after the retirement move, cancer struck Gwen, and so Kathy had temporarily moved in to nurse her mother during treatment. On one such evening, Kathy had helped get Gwen's nausea under control, put the exhausted woman to bed, and then tiptoed to the living room. She turned on the television, and saw a local news story regarding the twentieth anniversary of a murder that shattered the community's innocence. It was the first Kathy had heard of the tragedy, and she was fascinated to learn that it had occurred on her last day in town as a child.

When the victim's picture appeared on the screen, fascination turned to horror— one of those moments when Kathy regretted her unique talent. Though she'd never been formally introduced to the girl, she recognized her instantly, and she remembered seeing someone with her on that day, shortly before Kathy had climbed into the packed van with her family for the long drive to Halifax.

In the present-day courthouse, Kathy shuddered and let out a quiet whimper.

Becky put her book down and took her sister's hand. "You okay?"

"A little flashback." Kathy took a sip of bottled water. "Unfortunately, it led to the thought that I could have been the victim."

"That's it." Becky reached into her pocket and retrieved a deck of cards. "You need a diversion. What do you want to play?"

"Fine. Something mindless—crazy eights."

While Becky shuffled the cards, Kathy said, "I *so* appreciate you being here with me."

"I know you'd do it for me."

Kathy checked her watch and sighed. "In theory, I understand the rationale for keeping me out here while other

The Cursed Memory

evidence is presented. But it's a bit of a joke in this case because the lawyer told me it would largely be a rehashing of the same circumstantial evidence presented at the original trial, most of which I either watched in that news documentary or read on the public record."

Becky began dealing the cards, each one snapping as she pressed them onto the cushioned seat between them.

Kathy thought about the key facts she had learned: at approximately 11:30 am, Janet was last seen alive, leaving her friend's house in town on the way home for lunch; at 12:35 pm, David Parsons, a nineteen-year-old local had been pulled over for speeding, headed South on highway 21 into town. The officer who pulled him over reported that Parsons seemed suspiciously frightened; At 1:20 pm, a hiker found Janet's body 6 km north of town, behind an abandoned cabin in the bush, 100 meters from Highway 21.

Parsons had initially claimed he had been out for a drive with no particular destination, on a day off from his warehouse job. However, under intense cross examination, he panicked and changed his story, explaining that he was returning from a drug deal in London, ninety minutes away. Investigators did find drugs in his car, but Parsons was unable to come up with a name or contact information for his supplier, whom he'd allegedly found randomly on a London Street.

Not only did Parsons lack an alibi for his whereabouts but a physical examination revealed lesions on his penis—consistent with difficult penetration—and a fresh scratch mark on his throat. When asked to explain the injuries, he collapsed in an emotional breakdown, and was ultimately found guilty and sentenced to life.

A clicking noise brought Kathy back to the present, and she noticed her sister's fingers snapping. "Hello?" said Becky.

"Sorry." Kathy picked up her cards and sorted them.

Becky turned over the top card on the deck, and said, "Hearts."

Kathy played the three of hearts. "I quite like the defense lawyer, and I know what she'll ask. It's the Crown lawyer that scares me. I'm told he can be a real prick to defense witnesses."

Becky played a card. "Don't worry about it. Just tell the truth and you'll be fine."

The door opened and the bailiff's head poked into the hall. "They're ready for you."

As they entered the courtroom, Kathy tried not to look at anyone until she was sworn in and seated on the witness stand. She glanced at Becky in the front row, and then scanned the gallery, wondering who was there in support of the accused and who for the victim—in other words, who was rooting for Kathy and who loathed her.

She then looked at the defense lawyer, Brenda Cairns, a slender woman about Kathy's age, wearing thick glasses. In discussions with Kathy before the trial, she seemed compassionate, knowledgeable, and poised; but in the courtroom, she sat perched on the edge of her seat as though reconsidering her career. Kathy wondered if it was her first solo trial.

"Your witness," said the judge.

Cairns stood and approached the witness stand. A sheet of paper trembled as she handed it to Kathy. "Miss Staynor, can you please confirm that this document is addressed to you."

Kathy read the first few lines and handed it back. "It is."

"Thank you." Cairns turned to the judge. "Your Honour, I am holding an expert witness report that I would like to submit as evidence."

Hawkins nodded and the court clerk took the sheet from Cairns and walked it to the judge.

"In this document," said Cairns, "Dr Ian Kirch, head of Neuropsychology at the University of Toronto, confirms that

The Cursed Memory

Kathy Staynor was diagnosed with Hyperthymesia, a rare condition marked by exceptional memory for personal history. It's also known as Highly Superior Autobiographical Memory, or HSAM."

"Ms. Staynor," said Cairns, "please explain to the court how your memory differs from that of the average person."

Kathy cleared her throat and shifted in her seat.

"I can remember pretty well every day of my life since the age of nine."

"Excuse me," said Judge Hawkins, "but did you say you remember *every* day?"

"Pretty much."

"That's quite a claim. I'm surprised I haven't heard of this condition before," said Hawkins.

"It's extremely rare," said Kathy.

"How does it work? Do you see a giant calendar in your mind?"

"Not like your typical calendar with rows and columns; it's more like a long path that I walk along in my mind, and if I focus on an event, I can gradually fill in the surrounding details."

"Hmpf," said Hawkins. "Okay, Counsel, please continue with your examination."

"Thank you, Your Honour," said Cairns. "I'd like to demonstrate Ms. Staynor's ability to the court, by…"

"Your Honour," interrupted Deakin as he rose to his feet, "I'm concerned that Defense Counsel is about to ask the witness skill-testing questions that they could easily have rehearsed together before the trial."

Hawkins turned to Cairns, "Is that your plan, Counsel—were you going to quiz her?"

"No, Your Honour. I was planning to demonstrate the strength of her memory by asking *you* to test her."

Hawkins's eyebrows arched. "Me?"

"Yes, Your Honour. You're a *neutral* party, so feel free to google any significant day between 2002 and today, and ask her about it."

Hawkins scratched his chin for a moment. Then he turned to the keyboard on his bench and typed a few words. He turned back to the witness. "Ms. Staynor, when was Stephen Harper first elected Prime Minister?"

Kathy looked at the floor, her eyes twitching back and forth. "Let me see…I was eating breakfast with my father when he told me the election results. Hmmm…It was in January, and it was snowing, and we were eating early because he was going to drive me to band practice before school, so it was a Tuesday…and since he was talking about the results from the night before, that would make it Monday, Jan 23, 2006."

Deakin rocked forward, hands on his desk, eyes darting between witness and judge.

The judge looked sideways at Deakin for a moment, then turned back to his computer, typed a few words, and then said, "Ms. Staynor, what was the exact date of the 2008 Super Bowl? Who won? And by what score?"

Kathy paused for a moment, then looked at Hawkins, "I don't know."

"Why not?"

"My memory isn't encyclopedic; it's autobiographical. I only remember things that I observed, and I'm not a football fan, so I wouldn't have paid attention to the Superbowl. I'm a Blue Jays fan though."

Hawkins's fingers tapped on his keyboard. "What was the outcome of the Blue Jays game on August 26, 2012?"

"August 26, 2012," said Kathy as her eyes searched the air, "…Okay, I do remember watching that with my boyfriend at the time. I think they beat the Yankees."

"Your Honour," Deakin was on his feet again, "we've all heard of trivia buffs that memorize sports scores and people who study meticulous personal diaries, so, with all due respect, if there is to be any testing of the witness's capacity for recollection, should it not be done by a qualified professional in a controlled environment?"

Hawkins pulled at his beard and looked skyward for a minute, then nodded. "Sustained. I can appreciate Crown Counsel's concern, so I'd like to request that the Court Reporter strike my trivia questions from the record." He turned back to Cairns. "Counsel, please resume your examination of the witness."

Cairns walked across the floor and displayed a photograph of the victim for the judge and jury, then she presented it to Kathy. "Do you recognize this person, Ms. Staynor?"

"I do."

"Was she an acquaintance?"

"No, I just saw her occasionally at the park, and someone told me her name was Janet Harkness."

"Which Park specifically?"

"Oliver Switzer Park in Goderich."

"Any particular reason you remember her?"

"I was envious of her at the time because I was a skinny ten-year-old with braces, and she was a bit older and developed. I thought she was quite beautiful."

"Can you tell us when you last saw Janet in person?"

"May 12, 2002."

"Was there anything special about that day that helps you remember?"

"Yes, it was the day my family moved to Nova Scotia."

"Please tell us the details you remember about that day, and, in particular, anything you saw related to Janet."

Kathy cleared her throat. "As I mentioned, it was my last day in Goderich, and my mother let me go to the park mid-morning for a final visit with my friend Marissa. It was a relatively new park at the time, on the edge of town next to a farm field where a subdivision was slated for development. As usual, my friend and I met under the arch of a statue at the southeast corner because it was a fun hiding place with peep holes that allowed me to spy on other people. It wasn't normally a busy park, and that morning it was completely deserted, probably because a storm was forecast—my mother told me later that she'd been too busy packing to check the weather.

"Anyway, I remember seeing Janet pass by on a bicycle, and then I heard a man's voice call her name, so I peeked out and saw her cycle over to a white car—a hatch back—at the edge of the park where the forest begins. I briefly saw the man through the open driver's window. He had light brown hair, a thin face and a blue shirt, and he must have known Janet because I heard him say that there was a big storm coming and she'd never get back to her house before it hit, so he offered her a lift. I figured it was a neighbor or friend of her family, so I sat back down. I heard a bit of noise that sounded like he was putting the bike in the trunk, and, at that same time, Marissa spied my mom's car pull into the parking lot at the opposite end of the park. I also remember the wind picking up and we saw storm clouds coming in, so we sprinted to my mom. She took a final picture of us together, then we dropped Marissa off and went home to finish packing for the trip."

"I realize the man you saw in that car has aged twenty years," said Cairns, "but can you identify him in this courtroom,".

Kathy looked at Parsons: stone-faced, jet-black hair, heavy-boned, and sitting next to a guard. She then glanced at the jurors and the gallery, and then turned back to Cairns. "No."

"When did you become aware of Janet's death?"

"May of this year."

"It was national news in 2002. Nobody told you about it?"

"I asked my mother that same question before she died,

and she said they did hear about it, but they decided it might be too upsetting for someone my age."

"Your friend Marissa didn't tell you?"

Kathy started to glance at the gallery, but then caught herself. "No. I tried to contact her to chat a couple of times in 2002 after we moved, but she never returned my calls."

"How *did* you learn of Janet's death."

"After my mother moved back to Goderich for retirement, she was diagnosed with cancer. One night when I was here caring for her, I saw a news story about the 20th anniversary of the murder."

"Thank you," said Cairns. "No further questions at this time, Your Honour."

As Cairns took her seat, the judge nodded to the Crown lawyer, "Your witness."

Deakin appeared to be about fifty, with salt and pepper hair and a gentle face—more Mr. Rogers than Perry Mason. Sitting with his shoulders back, chin raised, he nodded to the judge, then stood and approached the witness stand with a relaxed smile and said, "Given that I can't remember the colour of tie I wore last Sunday, I'm anxious to learn a bit more about your exceptional memory, Ms. Staynor. When did you first realize you had this special ability?"

"When I was fifteen."

"And how far back does your detailed memory go—to what year?"

"To when I was nine years old, which would be 2001."

"Are you aware of any reason it started then and not earlier?"

"I think it relates to being bullied when we first moved to Goderich, because I started spending a lot of time focusing on happy memories as a coping mechanism."

"And in what year were you officially diagnosed with HSAM?"

"In 2009."

"I see. That presumably explains your sudden popularity online around that time, because a quick internet search using your name reveals your participation in news interviews, talk shows, and a couple of Netflix documentaries. You even had a little side business, hiring yourself out to be quizzed at different events. Isn't that right?"

"Yes."

"But, based on that same internet search, it appears your celebrity seemed to peter out approximately four years ago. Why is that?"

Kathy shrugged. "I guess the novelty wore off."

Deakin folded his arms. "You participated in a radio interview on Dec 10th, 2018. I presented a transcript of it to the jury. Do you remember that interview?"

After staring at the ceiling for a moment, Kathy's cheeks began to feel hot. "Yes, I remember it."

"I must say that was a very informative interview," said Deakin. "In it, you explained that 2018 was a rough year for you: diagnosed with obsessive compulsive disorder; bouts of anxiety and depression; and your brief marriage failed. Is that correct?"

"Objection," said Cairns as she rose from her chair. "Your Honour, I fail to see the relevance of the witness's personal life four years ago to today's trial."

"Your Honour," said Deakin as he held out empty hands, "my question is necessary to establish a possible motive for the witness's testimony today.

"Objection overruled," said Hawkins. "Please answer the question, Ms. Staynor."

Kathy's eyes were stinging now. She swallowed, then squeaked, "Yes."

"Later in that same interview," continued Deakin, "you stated that you were offered medication to deal with your OCD, but that it would have the side effect of muting your memory skills somewhat. Do you remember that?"

The Cursed Memory

"Yes."

"Did you begin taking that medication in 2018?"

"Yes, I did."

"Are you still taking that medication now?"

"No."

"Approximately when did you stop taking the medication?"

"When I was helping my mother earlier this year."

"That was when you first learned of the murder, is it not?"

Kathy shrugged. "Yes."

"I see."

Kathy was becoming aware of an annoying connection: the faster she answered; the slower Deakin posed his questions, and if she slowed down, he sped up.

Deakin paced the floor slowly while admiring his shoes, then he abruptly turned to Kathy. "The jury watched excerpts from the documentaries you participated in between 2014 and 2016, and I must say you looked like you were having fun. Did you enjoy the fame…while it lasted?"

Kathy tilted her head from side to side. "Well…there were…"

"Please answer with a simple 'yes' or 'no'. Did you enjoy the fame while it lasted?"

Kathy squeezed her hands together. "Yes." She caught a glimpse of Cairns rolling her eyes.

Deakin nodded a few times, then resumed pacing. "Your old friend Marissa was on the witness stand before you, and she *did* remember being with you on the day you packed up and left for Nova Scotia. She even vaguely remembers sitting under the statue with you that morning. However, she did *not* remember seeing Janet at all in the park that day. Does that surprise you?"

Once again, Kathy had to resist looking at the gallery. "As I mentioned earlier, I've got a condition that allows me to remember more detail in long term memory than do most people."

"A simple 'yes' or 'no', please Ms. Staynor. Does it surprise you that Marissa doesn't remember seeing Janet in the park that day?"

Kathy exhaled heavily. "No."

"Earlier today, you told the court that you tried unsuccessfully to contact Marissa during the month after you moved east in 2002. Have you spoken to her since then?"

Kathy swallowed. "Yes, after I saw the twentieth anniversary news story, I found her on the internet and then contacted her." Kathy glanced at Cairns, who was massaging her temples while looking down at her desk.

"And this recent communication with Marissa," said Deakin, "occurred before you contacted the police?"

"Yes."

Deakin's eyebrows arched, then his head snapped back theatrically. "You contacted Marissa *before* contacting the police." He stared silently at Kathy for thirty seconds, then finally said, "I know you moved away from Goderich on May 12, 2002, Ms. Staynor, but did you have any reason to believe that Marissa was moving away from Goderich on that same day?"

"No."

"Then, if Marissa was living in Goderich after you left, I'm sure we can agree that she would have heard about the murder of Janet ad nauseum from that day onward—'yes', or 'no'?"

"Yes."

"And, if Marissa had seen Janet with a stranger that morning, would you not expect she would have reported that information to an adult the moment she learned of Janet's murder?"

"That makes sense, but I …"

Deakin interrupted, "'Yes', or 'no'?"

"Yes."

"Perhaps you lacked confidence in your own recollections. Is that why you called Marissa?"

"No."

"Well, the only other reason I can think of for you to contact Marissa twenty years later would be to plant *your* version of events in her mind."

Kathy's eyes darted to the jury and then back to Deakin "No," she said louder than intended.

"Ms. Staynor," said Judge Hawkins, "please refrain from speaking until you're asked a question."

Deakin folded his arms and paced in front of the witness. "This trial concerns very serious crimes. Would you agree, Ms. Staynor?"

"Yes."

"And would you agree that it's not every day that someone who's spent twenty years in prison is pronounced innocent?"

"Yes."

"Then can we agree that if the accused is exonerated in this case, it would become high profile national news?"

"Objection, Your Honour," said Cairns. "The question is speculative."

Judge Hawkins probed his cheek with a tongue, then said, "Objection overruled. Please answer the question, Ms. Staynor."

Cairns' mouth hung open as she sank bank into her seat while staring at the judge.

Deakin cleared his throat, then repeated, "Would you agree that an exoneration in this case would be high profile news, Miss Staynor— 'yes', or 'no'?"

Kathy hesitated. "I suppose...yes."

Deakin nodded several times, then turned to Hawkins. "No further questions, your Honour."

Hawkins looked to Cairns. "Anything else from Counsel?"

Cairns stood and walked to the witness stand.

"Ms. Staynor, can you elaborate on why you contacted Marissa twenty years after the murder?"

"When I realized I had information to share, I got very anxious and I instinctively reached out to the only other witness I knew was at the park with me. In hindsight, it wasn't a great decision on my part, but I guess I thought there was a remote possibility she'd seen something as a little girl, but nobody believed her. Regardless, in no way did I intend to influence Marissa. I'm constantly faced with people that don't remember things the way I do, so I've learned not to push my recollections on them." She looked down and watched a tear hit the floor. "In some ways it's a curse having HSAM."

While the bailiff offered a box of tissues to Kathy, Cairns said, "No more questions at this time, Your Honour."

Hawkins turned to Deakin. "Any further questions for the witness from Crown Counsel?"

"No further questions, Your Honour," said Deakin.

"Well," said Hawkins, "given that both counsels have indicated they have no further questions for you, I'd like to thank you for your participation, Ms. Staynor. You're free to leave."

"Thank you," said Kathy.

Hawkins pulled back his sleeve and squinted at his watch. "I'd like to call a lunch break at this time. We'll reconvene at one pm." The judge stood and walked to his chamber, eliciting murmurs from the gallery as observers filed out of the courtroom.

While the guard escorted the accused to a side door, Parsons's tired eyes met Kathy's for a moment and seemed to say, 'Thanks for trying.'

Kathy turned and walked to the gallery, where she got a hug from her sister.

"I screwed that up," said Kathy.

"You did fine," said Becky. "I don't know how the blood-sucking Prosecutor sleeps at night."

The Cursed Memory

"Yeah, I'm not used to having my character assassinated in public. Anyway, I need a toilet before my bladder explodes."

They left the courtroom and walked down the hallway to a public restroom. While Becky waited outside, Kathy used the toilet, then washed her hands and face. After patting her face dry with a paper towel, she leaned on the counter and looked deep into the eyes staring back in the mirror.

Kathy could remember every hurtful thing done to her in the last 21 years. Even minor conflicts were visible in such detail she could emotionally relive them. To cope with that ever-growing burden of bad memories, she had learned the virtue of forgiveness, and given that she would remember all the hurts again tomorrow, forgiving was a daily ritual.

Kathy smiled at the mirror, and whispered, "You're forgiven, Mr. Deakin."

As she stepped into the hallway, Becky asked, "What would you like to do now?"

"I'm starving."

"Great. Name your food— my treat."

"I noticed a place close by."

"Lead the way."

They left the courthouse and crossed the street to a small shop where they ordered sandwiches and iced tea. Kathy said to the cashier, "Take out, please."

"Do you want to eat at the condo?" asked Becky.

"Actually, I'd like to eat at the park."

"You mean ... *the* park?"

Kathy nodded. "It's not far."

While Becky drove, Kathy watched familiar sites through the window for a minute and then said, "I had an awful time resisting looking for Marissa in the gallery. Did you recognize her from the Facebook page I showed you?"

"Yes, but when the lawyer grilled you about contacting her, she got up and left."

Kathy shook her head. "You've heard my sermons on

forgiveness, but there's something else about HSAM that I find even more difficult, and I don't think I ever told you about it."

"What's that?"

"I remember all the events in my friends' lives. Whether it's the date they divorced or the date their goldfish died, I'll call them on that anniversary to let them know I care."

"Your friends are very lucky."

"Yeah, but everyone forgets *me*! I realize their brains aren't wired like mine, but it really hurts sometimes."

Kathy fished a tissue from her pocket, then blew her nose. "I don't just remember the date I found Daddy dead in the garage; I remember the smell, the dried blood on the floor, and even the feel of his cold skin when I touched him. On every July 25 since then, I relive that nightmare… alone… because my phone never seems to ring on that day."

Becky took one hand off the wheel and placed it on her sister's knee. "I'm so sorry. I never thought about it that way."

Kathy put her face in her hands and sobbed. "I'm sick of having a perfect memory."

Becky pulled over and stopped the car. She held her sister and said, "Maybe we shouldn't go to the park."

"No," said Kathy. "Believe me, I wish I could forget it, but I can't. So, I'd like to face it one last time and make peace with what happened."

WHEN THEY ARRIVED at the park, Kathy shuddered. She took a deep breath, then got out and led Becky to a bench, where they sat and unwrapped their sandwiches.

Kathy pointed up at towering trees. "Those were puny when we lived here." She sipped her drink, then nodded to a weathered statue. "That's where Marissa and I used to hide."

The Cursed Memory

Kathy pivoted 180 degrees and gestured to the parking lot. "And over here is where Mom…" She trailed off.

"Where Mom what?" asked Becky. "Kathy?"

Kathy's mouth hung open as she looked alternately at the parking lot and the road several times. Then she rewrapped her sandwich and said, "I need to see something at Mom's place."

KNEELING on the floor in the condo storage locker, Kathy checked the labels on binders in a cardboard banana box.

Becky leaned over her shoulder. "Can I help?"

"No, I think I found it."

Kathy extracted a binder. While flipping through its pages, she abruptly stopped and jabbed a photo with her finger. "There. It exists." She fumbled in her jacket pocket for reading glasses, then put them on. After studying the page, she seized Becky's arm. "I have to get back to the trial."

"What?"

Kathy sprang to her feet and closed the locker door. "Come on. I'll explain on the way."

They hurried outside and jumped into the car. As Becky drove, Kathy reopened the binder and explained, "Mom took a picture of Marissa and me as we ran over to her in the park, but she didn't get prints made until we were settled in Halifax a couple of months later, and, by then, I wanted to forget Goderich, so I never looked at the photos. When you and I were cleaning up the condo for the real estate agent, I saw 'Goderich 2001-2002' written on the album cover, but I still didn't open it."

"What made you look now?"

"At the park today, I envisioned Mom taking our picture as we ran toward her, so I lined up the statue with where Mom stood … and look." Kathy pulled a photo out of its protective sleeve and held it up beside the steering wheel.

Becky's eyes flicked back and forth between the road and the photo. "It's hard to focus while I'm driving. What am I looking for?"

Kathy placed a finger on the photo. "Right here, in the background between the statue and a tree, you can see the back of someone getting into the driver's seat of a white car, and you can see a passenger looking through the rear window."

"They're really small in the picture," said Becky. "Are you sure it's her?"

"It has to be. It was the only car there when we ran over to Mom."

"You can't see the man's face from that angle."

"No. But you can sort of see the license plate." Kathy slumped back into her seat. "And in my mind's eye, I can see him clearer than ever: light hair, thin face and a really pronounced cleft in his chin … almost cartoonish, like buttocks.

———

MINUTES LATER, Becky parked at the courthouse, and they hurried up the steps. As they walked into the gallery, Hawkins invited the Prosecutor to present closing arguments.

The sisters sat in the front row, a few steps from Cairns. Kathy cupped a hand over Becky's ear. "I don't want to interrupt Deakin, but, when he finishes, I'll show it to Cairns."

Deakin stood in front of the jury. "I'd like to thank you, members of the jury, for your participation in this important case. Rape and murder are extremely serious crimes, and given the severity of the punishment in such a case, one would expect the accused, if innocent as claimed, would have amassed credible supporting evidence over the last twenty years. However, we've seen no new physical evidence or theories of an alternative killer. Instead, we've listened to two weak testimonies. The first, a lone pathologist disputing the testimony of two experienced peers who concurred in 2002 that lesions photographed on the accused were inflicted on the day of Janet Harkness's murder. The second, a washed-up carnival act trying to leverage this tragedy to rekindle her former celebrity. Twenty years and that's all defense can come up with…"

As Deakin droned on, Kathy looked away and made a mental note to forgive him doubly tomorrow, then her gaze fell to the photo in her lap. A minute later, she felt a jab in her ribs.

"The Prosecutor's finished," whispered Becky. "Go."

Kathy tiptoed up to Cairns who was about to present defense's closing arguments. Kathy slid the photo onto the table in front of Cairns and whispered, "I found something else—something important."

The startled lawyer looked at the photo and then at Kathy. "What is this?" she hissed. "We can't submit evidence at this point."

"What's going on here?" asked Hawkins.

"I'm sorry, Your Honour," said Cairns. This witness wanted to share some potential photographic evidence, and I was just trying to explain to her…"

"This is irregular," snapped Hawkins. "Counsels, I'll see you both in my chamber, and bring this new exhibit with you. Court will take a ten-minute recess."

The judge disappeared through a doorway behind the bench, his gown flowing and both lawyers following close behind.

Kathy slunk back to her seat next to Becky and grimaced. "He sure looked upset."

THE JUDGE DROPPED into a chair and glared across his desk at the attorneys. "I've had witnesses break protocol before, but this is the first time I've seen an attorney blurt in front of the whole courtroom during closing arguments that there's more evidence. You should have approached the bar to confer with me in private."

"I apologize, Your Honour," said Cairns.

Hawkins sighed. "Look, I'm only months away from retirement, and I'd like to finish my career without leaving any baggage behind, so, rather than call a mistrial, I'm going to instruct the jury to ignore any mention of new evidence. Are we in agreement with that?"

Both attorneys nodded.

"Alright," said Hawkins. "Now, *off the record*, what is this evidence anyway?"

Cairns placed the photograph on the desk between them.

Hawkins lifted his glasses and studied the picture, then arched his eyebrows and scowled at Cairns. "That's what this is all about?" He shoved the photo aside. "I'm starting to question the sanity of your witness, Cairns, so I hope to hell you don't consider encouraging an appeal for another Goddamned retrial based on some grainy photo of a random car."

"I respectfully disagree, Your Honour." Cairns slid the photo back to the center of the desk and turned it 90 degrees. "The witness and her friend are clear in the foreground, the inlaid date lines up with the date of the murder, and..." Cairns pointed to the car. "Even with my poor eyesight, I can see someone looking through the back window, and I can make out a couple of the fuzzy digits on the license plate. With proper enhancement in a lab, this might be compelling."

Cairns picked up the photo and slipped it into her pocket.

The Cursed Memory

Kathy stared at the door concealing the lawyers and judge. As she imagined their reactions to the photo, her eyes narrowed, then she pulled out her phone and performed a search. As she thumbed through the results, she felt numb and grabbed her sister's arm. "We need a whole new trial, with a new judge and jury."

"What do you mean?" asked Becky.

The door to the judge's chamber opened, and Kathy's grip tightened on her sister's arm. She watched the two lawyers return to the courtroom, exchanging shrugs before diverging toward their respective tables. Cairns took her seat and held her forehead.

Kathy turned to whisper to Becky, but a deafening bang ripped through the quiet courtroom. The guard hustled the accused out the side door, jurors clamouring behind them.

The lawyers and observers in the gallery scrambled toward the rear exit while frantically scanning for the source of the gunshot.

Becky crouched beside her chair, yanked on Kathy's arm and shrieked, "Come on. We've got to get out."

But Kathy remained seated and watched the bailiff run to the open door of the judge's chamber, where he covered his mouth with a hand and leaned against the doorframe for support.

Kathy turned her phone to show Becky a picture of a man with a deeply cleft chin. "That's what he looked like when he became a judge 18 years ago… before the beard and glasses."

About Peter Smith

Peter Smith has an eclectic and ever-evolving mix of interests. His debut novel, *The Mantis and the Monarch*, explores the fascinating, yet chaotic, world of cancer research.
 On cold winter nights, he can be found sitting in front of a fire on a small family farm in Ontario, Canada, trying to capture his imagination with pen and paper. Peter can always be reached by email at fairweatherfarming@gmail.com

Walking after Midnight

Merja Tammi

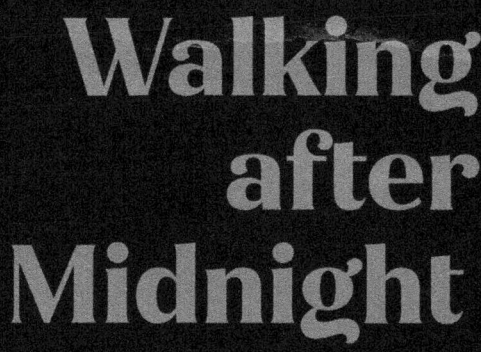

Detective Koski had his man, but an inexperienced prosecutor and a flimsy lie allowed the killer to go free. Now a vigilante killer is doing what Martin couldn't. Should he pursue the case or let the vigilante do his worst?

I go out walkin' after midnight
Out in the moonlight
Just like we used to do.
I'm always walkin.'
After midnight,
Searchin' for you.

Sung by Patsy Cline
Written by Alan Block and Don Hect

Walking after Midnight

Merja Tammi

F rom my perch, high in the hills, I observe darkness swallowing the dusk. Imperceptibly, tiny lights appear, like jewels stitched onto a black velvet gown. Patsy Cline winds down her song, and I rouse myself to prepare for the hunt.

By midnight, when most of the good citizens of Vancouver are asleep, others emerge onto the glittering streets. It's a Friday night and drivers are busy. My driver, Raoul, tells me he hopes for good fares. The best he can hope for is that no one vomits poor judgment over carpeted floorboards.

Raoul complains about the 'youth of today.' Let him drone on. His life is short, and, if the poet is to be believed, nasty and brutish. We are all here for a short time. Few things we do truly matter. Except what I do. What I do matters.

THE BEDROOM DOOR creaked and the sound roused Sarah.

"Rise and shine, Hon. Come and have breakfast before your exam."

Sarah opened her eyes, still clutching the book she had fallen asleep reading. Her mother lifted it out of her hands.

"You've been up reading *Poetry of the Romantics*? How does this topic relate to nursing?"

"It's an elective, Mom, and kind of interesting."

Angela's brows furrowed as she read from the book:

"For the Romantics, individualism was greater than society. The movement was a reaction to the industrial revolution, and valued love and nature above science. They believed in the innate goodness of the individual."

Sarah laughed, "I guess they never met the people you and Dad deal with."

"You're too young to be cynical. Now get up and have some food."

Sarah ran a comb through her hair then followed Angela to the kitchen. Sitting down at the kitchen table, Sarah bent down to pat their retriever, Sunny.

"How was your night, Dad?"

Martin Koski ran his fingers through his thinning gray hair. He released a deep sigh before answering. "It was a rough one."

Angela came up behind her husband and rubbed his shoulders, then bent down to kiss him on the top of his head.

"They're really getting their money's worth out of you— right to your last week of work," she said.

Martin drew his wife's hand from his shoulder and gently kissed it.

"Yeah, but then we ride off into the sunset, darlin.'"

Sarah smiled and shook her head. "It better happen, Dad, you've been promising Mom this trip for a very long time."

"Oh, he's doing it," Angela said, "but now I'm off. I need to be at the office before my first client beats me there."

Sarah watched her mom pull on her overcoat and grab her keys and briefcase. "Have a great day, Mom."

"You too," she said, and left.

Sarah turned to her father. His eyes were shadowed, and the whites hinted at his exhaustion.

"I saw it on the news. How bad was it?"

"Pretty bad."

"They're calling him the box cutter killer. Seems like an odd choice for a weapon."

"Not really. I've seen a kitchen fork used as a weapon. A utility knife is an easy thing to hide, and it can cut through skin, tendon, muscles, and blood vessels and, if the killer knows basic anatomy, death can be damn quick."

Sarah pushed her chair back from the table and stood up. "I'm sorry it had to be you at the scene Dad. Who was the victim? They never said a name."

"Remember Barnett?"

"Oh God," Sarah said and sat back in her chair. "You mean the guy who killed Vicky Wakefield and those other girls last year?"

"That's the guy. Tony and I had him. He got off because his mother gave him an alibi. A good prosecutor would have cut through her story, but we weren't that lucky. It was some new kid, just promoted, didn't know his ass from a hole in the ground. Tony took early retirement after that case."

"Why'd he quit?"

"He found the bodies. He has a granddaughter the same age. It was too much. Still, it surprised me that he took a job doing security at a parking lot."

"Turned out for me though since he hired me. He talks about some of the cases you guys handled."

Martin drained his coffee mug and brought it down hard on the table and rose.

"Well, enough chitter chatter. You have an exam, and I have work. See you at dinner, Kiddo."

"Sure, you too, Dad. Go fight the good fight."

Sarah watched her father copy his mother's moves as he pulled on his coat, grabbed his keys, and left.

Sarah poured herself another cup of coffee and headed up the stairs, humming a song. Sunny followed close behind.

It isn't hard to kill. The body has seven zones vulnerable to attack. The most effective is slicing into the carotid artery, but the kill needs to be up close. I looked Barnett in the eye. I never looked away, even as I struck. Before he knew what I was going to do, I pushed the edge of the blade into his razor burned red neck, then pulled across. I made sure to get between the neck muscles, otherwise there could have been a struggle.

He grabbed his throat and staggered back. Blood seeped through his fingers, and he fell to his knees. When he looked up at me, I could see the confusion in his eyes. "It's for the girls" I said.

The night had turned cold, and steam rose from his blood as it left his body, as if his life force was rising from his carcass. He died in twenty-five seconds.

I never leave evidence. I'm good at hiding my tracks.

THAT EVENING, when Martin returned home, Angela was sitting at the table, sipping a glass of wine, rubbing Sunny behind the ears, and Sarah was standing in front of microwave.

"I'm reheating some lasagna, Dad, are you okay with that?"

"Lovely," Martin said, "and looks like there's wine to go with it." Angela placed a goblet in front of her husband and filled it.

"Catch any bad guys?" Angela asked.

"Not today. How about you?"

"Well, I made sure a guy is going to pay alimony and child support. Does that count?" Angela said and took another sip of wine.

"Absolutely. Anyone interesting?"

"Nope, just some shmuck who is very bad at hiding his money."

Sarah placed a plate in front of each parent, then loaded one for herself.

"Bon Appetit."

Later than evening, while Angela and Sarah watched *Legal Eagles*, Martin went into the office he shared with his wife and closed the door. One minute later, he was back out.

"Sarah, were you on my computer today?"

"Uh, yeah, I had to send in an assignment and my computer was acting up."

"Sarah, I've told you not to."

"Dad, all I did was send off my assignment."

"Still, Hon, stay off it, okay?"

"Okay, sure, I'm sorry, Dad."

Martin went back to his office and closed the door.

"Your father isn't angry at you, he's just on edge about Barnett. It's bothering me too."

"That was your last criminal case, wasn't it?"

"I did some work on it. I was upset Barnett got off. The evidence was overwhelming, and he should have been convicted." Angela sipped her wine, then added, "You weren't on my computer as well, were you?"

"Sure, Mom, I would love to know the intimate details of your alimony and child support evading client. Besides, you change your password all the time. Dad never does."

The women turned their attention back to the television, and Angela critiqued the show, and pointed out legal errors. At ten o'clock, Martin came out of the office.

"I'm off to bed."

"I'm coming up as well." Angela said.

Sarah turned off the television and said, "I'll let Sunny out and then I'm going to read a bit."

I LOOKED out into the night. Darkness had crept in without me noticing. Down in the heart of the city, was my next victim. She didn't know I was coming. When I see the light dimming in her eyes, I will tell her she did a bad thing. The monster was dead, but those responsible for his release had to be punished. Only when her blood flowed out of her in a gentle, dark stream, would I cross her off the list.

I don't go out every night. I take time to plan and assess. I must be careful not make mistakes or get sloppy. It's seductive, my calling, and it pulls at me.

I listen to Patsy. It's as if she's singing to me.

>And as the skies turn gloomy
>Night winds whisper to me

———

SARAH SPENT the next day studying, and after having dinner with her parents, she said, "I'm off," throwing her backpack on her shoulder and heading toward the door.

"Wait, Sarah," said Martin, "I'll give you a ride."

"No way, Dad, you just got home. With my bike, I'll be at the parking lot in half an hour."

"It's raining." said Martin, "Besides, I haven't seen Tony for some time. It would be nice to say hello."

On the ride to the parking lot, they talked about school and Sarah's plans after graduation.

"I wish you wouldn't work here, Sarah, especially night shifts."

"I am perfectly safe. Plus, a bad guy would have to get through the security lock and bulletproof glass."

Martin pulled up to the booth and waved to the man inside.

Tony grabbed his lunch bag and strolled toward Martin.

Sarah hopped out of the car, waved to her father, and got into the ticket booth.

"Marty, you never call, you never write. What brings you down here?"

"Hi Tony. Just making sure Sarah gets here safely."

"You worried about Barnett's killer?"

"You've heard?"

"I still have contacts in the force. Don't worry, Marty. Barnett's killer is not coming after us, or your kid. We did everything right. We had the psychopath in the bull's eye and if it wasn't for that snot-nosed prosecutor, Barnett would be rotting in a cell. Maybe it's better this way. Our tax dollars aren't going to waste."

"Tony, don't talk like that or you'll be in the frame."

"I'm just glad I don't have to be the guy trying to catch this vigilante. He's done the world a service. If it was me, Marty, I'd look the other way."

"There's a law. It has its flaws, but we can't just ignore it."

"I'm a civilian now, Marty. I don't have to hide my feelings."

"Soon I will be as well. I'm retiring in a few days, so someone else will have to catch the guy."

The men parted, and Martin waved to Sarah then drove away.

Alone in the booth, Sarah pulled out her textbook and coffee mug. She looked at the photos Tony had plastered on the short wall below the glass. Tony with his wife Jessie, Tony with his boys Carl and Frankie, and many more.

"You're one of the good guys." Sarah said to a picture of Tony holding his latest grandchild, then smiled as she looked through Tony's music list.

"I wouldn't have figured you for a Patsy Cline fan, Tony." Sarah said, then closed her eyes as she listened to the song as it echoed inside the cement walls.

A WOMAN, so ordinary I almost felt sorry for her, answered the door. It was very late, yet she let me in, believing what I told her.

"Hello." she said. It sounded more like a question than a greeting. She was older than I'd imagined. There was noise on the street, a couple walking their dog.

"Delivery," I said.

"Please, please, come in," she said.

I stepped into the shabby hallway, and closed the door.

"You're all wet. Let me make you a cup of tea."

We sat at a plain kitchen table. I allowed her to put a mug on the table in front of me. I never touched it. Her mug was faded, but it once said, 'Queen' in red letters.

"My boy got me this mug for my birthday, many years ago. I stood up and moved around the table. When she looked up, I stabbed, and I pulled. "You lied." I said, but I don't think she understood. "Your son tortured and killed five little girls, and you lied for him." Instead of grabbing for her throat, she tried to reach for the phone beside her mug. It fell to the floor, and I kicked it away. A needless action. She wouldn't have time to call anyone, however, she lasted longer than Barnett.

"MARTY, how come you're still up." Angela said as she came into the kitchen, pulling off her trench coat and draping it over a chair.

"You're just getting home now? Jeez, Angie, it's almost one o'clock."

"As I keep saying, if we are finally retiring, I have to make sure my case files are up to date."

"I couldn't sleep."

"Seems to be a lot of that going around," she said as Sarah came into the kitchen.

"Hey, how come you're both up?" Sarah asked.

"Old people get insomnia, Sweetie. How come you're up?"

"Can't sleep."

"Want something to eat?"

"Nah, I'm just grabbing a glass of milk and going back to bed."

Sarah started up the stairs but stopped when Martin spoke.

"Listen, Sarah, I was just saying to your mom that I shouldn't have been talking to you about the case. It was stupid of me."

"No, it's okay, Dad. It's interesting hearing both of you talk about your work."

Martin's phone rang. He answered, his grip tightening as he listened.

"I'll be there asap. Send me the address." He hung up, and said, "I have to go. Looks like we have another victim."

"Another bad guy down?" Sarah asked.

"No, Barnett's mother. Before Barnett was killed, she was going to recant her testimony."

"Too little, too late," said Sarah.

I'VE NEVER KILLED someone innocent. I never will. My targets are the ones who get away with the most heinous crimes. Small acts, moments of selfishness, greed, and looking the other way, are the true acts of evil. We are as culpable as the killer when we look the other way, and as guilty as the abuser when we fail to protect the vulnerable.

MARTIN PULLED on the offered coverall, gloves, and booties before entering the house. In the hallway, he saw a large floral arrangement on the console table. He pulled the card off the holder,

"Deepest condolence from all of us at Royal Oak Insurance." He read out, then handed it to a plainclothes officer who put it in a plastic bag. "Check this out. The florist, the name on the card, it could be a lead."

Blood had pooled around Carla Barnett's neck and around her head like a dark halo. Her arm was stretched out. She had tried to reach for her phone, lying several feet away. Two mugs of coffee were on the table. Forensics were busy with the body.

"Make sure you get any prints off the mugs."

"Marty, this isn't our first rodeo," said a thin, sandy-haired man kneeling over the victim.

"I know, Jackson, just making sure."

Martin looked around the kitchen. Old oak cabinets flanked a window shaded by faded curtains. The countertops, like the brown linoleum floor had many worn spots. On the brown refrigerator two cards of condolence and a fuzzy picture of a young boy were held on by magnets.

"Welcome to the eighties, where everything was harvest gold, avocado green, or brown." Martin said, then turned his attention back to the scene on the floor.

"What's the story, Jackson?"

"Body shows same wounds as on Barnett. Most likely the same killer. Nothing more I can do here. You'll get the full report tomorrow."

―――

The fog hides me and muffles my steps. There is one more name on my list. I stand outside the man's living room window. He lounges on his couch, bared chest, one hand down his pajama pants. He swirls the wine glass in his other hand, then raises it and drinks. His Adam's apple moves

upward as he gulps, the epiglottis sealing off the trachea, allowing him to drink without choking. When he opens the door, he says he's surprised to see me, but lets me in. I step close to him. Very close. I am holding my weapon behind my back. He's made my job easy.

"You let Barnett off. The evidence was all there. You never used it. You're a pathetic excuse for justice."

I thrust upward into his armpit to access the artery, then pull towards me.

His eyes searched out mine, then dimmed.

———

MARTIN TURNED from the stove and smiled at his wife and daughter when they came into the kitchen.

"There's the sleepy heads."

Sarah sniffed the air. "Fantastic, your famous ham and cheese omelets."

Martin's phone rang and he reached for it, but Angela took it and turned it off.

"No way. You are off the clock. Forever."

Martin laughed. "You're right. I did promise you, as of today, I'm leaving the crime-fighting to the next generation."

Sarah hugged her father. "Just go and enjoy yourselves. Go fishing, hiking, have a glass by the fire in the evening, or whatever else it is you guys want to do. I'll hold down the fort. Heck, you can even leave the dishes and I'll clean up after you."

———

FOR NOW, my work is done. I've answered the call.

———

Two hours later, after driving in silence, Angela was startled when Martin spoke, "Penny for them."

"Sorry, I guess I was 'away with the fairies' as Dad used to say."

"Yeah, for quite awhile, Hon. I don't mind. I just wondered what's going on with you?"

"Marty, you told Sarah you wanted to put Barnett away, but tell me the truth, doesn't some part of you feel justice was served when he was killed?"

"Ah, well, I suppose on the one hand the guy isn't going to be using up our tax dollars, as Tony said. Barnett should never have got off."

"No. he shouldn't have. And he didn't. Did he?" she replied as she slid a CD into the sound system.

"Jeez, Ang, I don't mind a little Patsy Cline, now and then, but you've been playing that same song over and over for a few weeks now."

"Sorry, Marty, I guess I have. I read that Cline didn't like the song, but it put her on the charts. I wonder if she got to like it after she had sung it so many times, or if she got sick of it?"

"Probably liked the money." Martin said.

"I guess we all do things we don't want to do, things that turn out for the best in the end. Right?"

"Right, and I'll listen to it now, if you promise not to play it again for a long time." Martin said, "and Angie?"

"Mmm?"

"I'm not just talking about the song. I mean all of it. It's over."

"Yes, Martin. I'm done." Said Angie and turned up the volume.

> I go out walkin' after midnight

Walking after Midnight

Out in the moonlight
Just hopin' you may be somewhere a-walkin'
After midnight, searchin' for you.

T̲h̲e̲y̲ ̲l̲i̲s̲t̲e̲n̲e̲d̲ to the final refrain, Patsy belting out a throaty "wa-wa-walking, wa-ooh-ah."

About Merja Tammi

Merja's work is influenced by the stark realism of novelists of her Scandinavian heritage, and the magic realism of writers from the Pacific West Coast of Canada.

Her writing explores the tension between the apparent normality of family life and the darker areas of humanity. With diplomas in business, sociology, and literature, as well as a career spent writing everything from technical manuals to school curricula, she is now enjoying writing for herself. Merja honed her short story writing skills at ice rinks while her husband coached, and her sons refereed and played competitive ice hockey.

She credits her Ottawa writing group, the Kanata Fiction Circle, with giving her the support and creative encouragement needed to take her writing to the next level.

You can reach Merja by email at MHTammiWrites@gmail.com.

Please leave a review!

If you enjoyed this collection of short stories could you please leave us a quick review? It would be very much appreciated!

You can leave a review on any or all of these sites:

Amazon

BookBub

Goodreads

Thank you!

About the KFC Scrutineers

The KFC Scrutineers is an Ottawa-based writing group whose members share creative goals and like-minded focus on reaching their personal artistic ideals.

Through critique, encouragement, and laughter, each contributor improves the other, uniting us in the written word.

The authors in the group hail from Canada, the USA, Finland and the Ukraine.

Watch for more stories from the group later this year.

Made in United States
North Haven, CT
02 September 2022